CH00905012

ESCAPE
FROM
AUSTRALWITZ

AW HALLIGAN

OCT 2001

© 2001 by A.W. Halligan. All rights reserved.

No part of this publication may be reproduced, stored in a retrieval system, or transmitted, in any form or by any means, electronic, mechanical, photocopying, recording, or otherwise, without the written prior permission of the author.

This novel is entirely a work of fiction. The names, characters and incidents portrayed in it are the work of the author's imagination. Any resemblance to acutal persons, living or dead, events or localities is entirely coincidental.

Cover Design by A.W. Halligan
This first publication is an unedited version.

National Library of Canada Cataloguing in Publication Data

Halligan, A. W. (Allan W.), 1957–
  Escape from Australwitz

   ISBN 1-55212-767-2

   I. Title.
PR9619.4.H34E82 2001   823   C2001-910731-5

TRAFFORD

This book was published *on-demand* in cooperation with Trafford Publishing.
On-demand publishing is a unique process and service of making a book available for retail
sale to the public taking advantage of on-demand manufacturing and Internet marketing.
On-demand publishing includes promotions, retail sales, manufacturing, order fulfilment, accounting
and collecting royalties on behalf of the author.

Suite 6E, 2333 Government St., Victoria, B.C. V8T 4P4, CANADA

Phone	250-383-6864	Toll-free	1-888-232-4444 (Canada & US)
Fax	250-383-6804	E-mail	sales@trafford.com
Web site	www.trafford.com	TRAFFORD PUBLISHING IS A DIVISION OF TRAFFORD HOLDINGS LTD.	
Trafford Catalogue #01-0167		www.trafford.com/robots/01-0167.html	

10   9   8   7   6   5   4   3   2   1

For my wife,

Anne

ESCAPE FROM AUSTRALWITZ

Alma stared at the large black egg in front of her.

She picked up the carving needle that looked like an ice pick, and began chipping a small hole in one end of the emu egg.

Let's hope it's the usual, she thought. I hate it when there's a dead chick inside. Blood and rotten gas are bad enough without having to look at dead things. Alma finished punching two small holes, one at either end of the egg. She stuck the carving needle upright into the wooden work-top of the bench.

Carefully leaning over the tin bucket beside her bench, she wrapped her dark lips around the hole at one end of the egg. She could feel the small hole with the tip of her tongue.

As she tilted one end of the egg down over the bucket, she blew hard and fast into the other end. Her cheeks puffed out tight. As the pressure built up, a clear bubble appeared at the other end. The bubble burst in a splutter. The liquid slowly oozed down into an already half-full bucket of slop - the result of nearly a full day's work.

When the egg was empty, she spat the salty taste from her mouth.

Alma picked up the needle again and began carving a picture of a kangaroo and bush scene into the black crinkly surface of the egg.

Then, as always, ever since she began working in the Aboriginal Tourism Centre - ten months ago - she let her mind go.

She began day-dreaming about the usual things - friends, family, the future and the past.

Alma looked up at the clock on the wall. Still thirty minutes to go.

She yawned and put the egg and carving needle down on the bench. Then she stretched her legs and leant forward to rest her head in the palm of her hand. Still feeling tired from no sleep last night Alma let her eyelids fall and wondered why she had been so restless in bed.

"Alma!" shouted the manager. He walked over and waited for the thirty or so other girls to leave before he continued talking. Alma felt very lonely when the last girl left.

"Lazy good for nothing Abos," scowled the red faced manager. "Wouldn't work in an iron lung."

He raked his fingers through his red hair and shook his head in disgust.

Alma looked at the dusty floorboards.

"I've given you two warnings already," he went on, "and you still won't listen. Well, that's it! You've got the sack."

The manager seemed on the verge of saying something else but Alma wasn't in the mood for waiting. She turned her back on him and walked out, closing the door behind her.

Stepping into the sunlight brought relief.

Not even one full year's work, just turned seventeen, and what happens? The sack!

She shook her head in disgust and walked off down the dirt road. It's not as if there would be any future in emu eggs, she thought. The extra food coupons did make her mother happy, though. What in hell would her mother say when she found out. Oh well, there's always dad's veggie garden - she could help him out.

Alma glanced at the electric fence surrounding the compound of Australwitz One. Ever since reading that book things just weren't the same anymore. Before finding that book, life in the compound was all that she had known! But now, she felt trapped. And only after one day and having read a couple of pages. How will I feel after I've finished the whole book?

Tin shacks lined the track. Naked children chased barking dogs, and more barking dogs chased screaming children.

The red dust puffed up around her sandals as she headed for home, each step setting off its own little exploding cloud of dry sand.

Only one day to turn her whole life upside down. It's that damn book! Spirit-beings, babies and birth. Spirit-beings sucked down into babies at birth.

She wondered what it would be like outside the compound. Australwitz One had shrunk somewhat, over the day, and Alma's idea of space had expanded so much that she now felt like a chook in a chookpen.

Trapped!

That shattering sensation of newly found knowledge still clung to her. Is it true though? How do I find out? That's not what they taught us at the Compound's primary school.

The old book, that she had discovered buried in the sand yesterday, told a different story to the one taught to her as a child.

She smiled at the puffs of fine sand shooting out from under her sandals. Her mind reached out with invisible arms - past the shanty shacks, through the electric fence, across the desert, over the mountains and far out beyond the great blue oceans.

"Alma!" came a voice from the dark shadows of a shack, "are you day-dreaming again?"

Alma turned and walked back to her long time friend, Old Shirley.

"Come in out of the sun and I'll make you a nice cup of tea," said the old woman.

Alma squinted and adjusted her eyes to the dark room.

Shirley sat in her favourite creaky cane chair. She moved her legs to allow Alma to squeeze past.

After the tea had been made they sat in silence, the only sounds heard were the occasional sips and slurps.

Eventually, Old Shirley was the first to speak:

"And how was your day, love?"

"Got the sack," giggled Alma.

"What happened?" Old Shirley laughed with her.

"Don't know," Alma shrugged her shoulders.

"Oh well," said Old Shirley, "you should be getting hitched up, especially at your age.

"Most girls are trying to have a baby, by this time. I don't know what to make of it. All these infertile girls! I think it has something to do with that weird hospital up there."

Old Shirley looked at the dirt floor and shook her head. After she thought it over for some time, she shook her head again.

"I just don't know what to make of it," she finally concluded.

"Shirley, what's it like outside?" Alma put her cup on the floor and leaned forward. "Tell me what it's like."

"I can't remember too well these days, Alma dear. That was over fifty years ago. What a name to be giving it. Fancy calling a Black's settlement 'Australwitz One', and that other one over near the Sacred Rock, 'Australwitz Two'. Stupid! Australwitz! I tell you, these modern people are crazy in the head. I've never heard anything so stupid.

"But, all the same, it's just as stupid for the Blacks to be calling this place a compound. It's more like a prison. No-one allowed in or out. Poor dear, seventeen years old and never once been out. Of course, it's different for me - I'm getting too old to worry about that anymore.

"What's brought all this on anyway? Getting the sack and now talking about the outside. Hmm?" Old Shirley looked concerned for a moment.

"What about those black rebels that are supposed to live on the outside - hiding out in the desert? How did they get out? How come no-one can catch them?" Alma leaned forward again. "Come on Shirl - tell me, will you?"

"You tell me who's been putting silly ideas in your head, and I'll go around and knock some sense into their thick black noggings," quipped Old Shirley.

They sat in silence for some time before Alma spoke again.

"I found a book, yesterday. Not one of those kiddies books from the school library. It was buried in the sand, about two miles out past the main canal. The wind had uncovered it. Some-one must've wrapped it in plastic and hidden it a long, long time ago."

"What sort of book?" Old Shirley screwed up her nose.

"It's a strange book. It talks of spirits and magic - does strange things to you, when you read it." Alma tried to smile.

Old Shirley stared at Alma for a bit, before talking.

"There used to be talk like that all the time - back in the old days, when I was your age. Not now though. You better keep it to yourself, love. Before you know it, the young ones will be laughing at you and calling you crazy.

"Then, zippetty bang! You'll be whizzed off up to that nut-house hospital, and seeing that crack-pot doctor. What's his name? I think it's Doctor Curr or something like that. You don't want to end up in that place, love. The next stop after that is the cemetery."

Alma thought it over, realising Old Shirley wasn't going to cough up any information today, and it would be better to try another time.

She said goodbye and continued on her way home.

About half a mile from home, the familiar smell of dope smoke came wafting over the air. A group of four boys stood in the middle of the road.

"Hey, looky looky," said the tallest. "It's Alma!"

"Want a smoke?" said another.

They all laughed.

Alma smiled and shook her head. She walked around the boys, keeping her gaze toward the ground.

One of the boys whistled after her.

"Oh, come on sugar," teased another.

"How about a jiggy-jig, then," yelled the tallest.

Another whistled.

Alma's attention went straight to her own body, and her thin white summer dress. She pulled at the hem, automatically. Embarrassed, she walked on at a faster pace.

Twenty yards from home, she passed her Aunt Wendy's shack. The tin wall rattled after someone banged it from the inside. It frightened Alma.

Aunt Wendy came running towards her. Blood trickled down her forehead. Her clothes were ripped.

"Alma, love!" Aunt Wendy rushed over and grabbed her arm.

"What's the matter?" asked Alma.

"He's gone crazy! It's the drink, again. Your Uncle Brumby has flipped his lid again."

By the look of her face, Uncle Brumby had been at it again. Alma put her arm around the frail, middle-aged woman, and coaxed her on toward their own place.

"Come with me to Mum's. She'll look after things," said Alma.

Alma could smell the sickening alcoholic fumes on her Aunt Wendy's breath and knew that Uncle Brumby wasn't the only black-hat.

"Get out of it, Alma. This is none of your business." Uncle Brumby shouted, staggering out of the shack.

He made a few half-hearted attempts at catching up, but soon collapsed in the middle of the road - bottle in hand.

Alma pinned Aunt Wendy to the side of the house.

"Mum!" she yelled. "Come quick. It's Aunt Wendy again."

Both her mother and father came to the call. Frank and Dulcy took Aunt Wendy inside.

Alma looked down at the blood splattered all over her dress.

She threw her hands into the air in frustration.

"That's it!" She shouted out to the blue sky above her. "I'm getting out of here. There's just got to be a way."

CHAPTER   TWO

Fred was having second thoughts about his chosen profession.

He stared at the white wall as he sat in the hospital canteen. Three months of on-the-job training, in the psychiatric wing of Australwitz One, were nearly finished. Soon he would have his qualifications - a one hundred percent certified psychiatrist.

A psychiatric textbook lay open in front of him, on the staff canteen table. The section that intrigued him was titled 'Electric Shock Treatment'.

Fred slowly shook his head from side to side. Something just wasn't quite right about it.

He moved his feet to allow a nurse to pass by. Stretching out his legs once more, he picked up a dictionary. Flicking through the pages, his thumb located the word - ECT.

He read the definition.

Electro Convulsive Therapy: To give electric shocks which cause convulsions.

He then flicked through towards the front of the dictionary.

Convulsions: Violent and uncontrollable movement of the body, shake violently, agitate, disturb.

Fred then flicked back towards the end of the dictionary. There it is, he thought.

Psychiatry: The study and treatment of mental disease.

Strange! He thought for a moment. Psyche means breath or life or soul. The bit on the end of the word, '-iatry' means healing. Therefore, from the word psyche-iatry, he figured that it meant, 'to heal the soul'.

That's very strange, he thought.

He wondered how electricity and drugs could heal the soul. I seem to be missing something, he thought.

"What's up?" said Nurse Shelley. "Having trouble with the crossword?"

She sat down across from Fred and sipped at her steaming drink.

"Nothing," said Fred. " I'm just catching up on the latest."

He ran his fingers through the black curly mop of hair on top of his head. Then he looked up at Nurse Shelley.

"Do you believe man has a soul, or that there could be a spiritual side to him?"

She laughed and then lit a cigarette.

"You're in the wrong building if you're looking for souls and spirits, Fred."

"I don't believe it," said Fred. "Four years in university and now this three month stint of on-the-job training, and I honestly don't think I'm the right man for the job."

He went on:

"Electric toasters, popping eyeballs and crazy drugs wasn't my idea of mending heads."

Nurse Shelley took a long deep draw on her cigarette as she eyed the trainee doctor of psychiatry.

"Look, Fred! One more week! All you have to do is stick it out for one more week and you're set for the rest of your life. You've already passed the exams. Doctor Curr will sign your competence certificate next week and that's that."

Fred looked at the tiles on the floor.

"Fred?" said Nurse Shelley.

He looked up.

"Finish the week, go for a holiday and then make a decision." She laughed and then stood up.

Fred watched her butt out the cigarette . He slowly stood up and followed the nurse out into the ward.

*

A couple of doors down the corridor Doctor Curr, the head psychiatrist and general manager of Australwitz One, sat at his desk. He rubbed his chin and pondered over the latest predicament.

Once again, there was another unexplained death in the psychiatric wing of the hospital.

He opened the top drawer and grabbed the bottle. He shook two little yellow tablets into his hand, hesitated and then added another three.

The cold coffee made him wince as he swallowed the pills.

Doctor Curr twiddled his gold-plated pen while staring at a speck of dust on the mahogany desktop.

He ran through his mind the events that happened before the recent death.

Right, now let's see. Patient was revived in the medical wing after an overdose from alcohol. Then sent to the psychiatric wing for observation when nervousness and anxiety set in. Patient was then given usual treatment of ECT and drugs. Dead the next day!

He thought about it for another ten seconds before dismissing the whole affair.

Anyway, the patient was over fifty years of age. Yes! That's it.

Must've been old age.

Doctor Curr pushed a button on his desk.

"Yes Doctor?" said the speaker.

"Are you ready for the rounds, Nurse Shelley?"

"Yes Doctor," said the speaker.

He joined the nurse at the reception desk.

As they strolled along the corridor, Doctor Curr planned out his day in silence. Tuesday morning. Let's see - one hour on the patient rounds, half an hour at the supply department, another half hour in the prison wing and then the rest of the day spent at the golf club in nearby Broken Hill. A smile spread across his face.

The patient rounds went according to plan, that is until they reached the last bed. That carefree smile soon disappeared at the sight of the new trainee doctor sitting on the side of the bed listening to a patient.

"It's these damn angels," muttered the young patient, sitting up in bed. "They keep talking to me. And then, when the night comes, they turn into devils - you know what I mean?"

Fred, the trainee doctor, turned and looked at Doctor Curr for advice. Both the patient and the nurse also looked at the doctor.

Doctor Curr stood in silence, so Fred began to speak:

"Jimmy seems to be getting lots of nightmares. What do you suggest, Doctor?"

"I never had these before, Doc," added Jimmy, brushing black curly locks away from the front of his eyes. His dark skin looked darker when contrasted with all the white of the hospital.

Doctor Curr first looked at the patient, then at the trainee doctor.

Finally, he turned to Nurse Shelley and said:

"Increase the dosage by the usual amount."

Nurse Shelley nodded before noting the change on the clipboard at the end of the bed.

"Thank you Doctor," said Jimmy, respectfully. "If it doesn't work, don't you worry. I can always go back on the plonk. Good tucker, that stuff! Cures every known ailment, you know."

Jimmy laughed briefly, before resuming his serious mood.

Doctor Curr and Nurse Shelley headed back to the reception desk, now that they had completed the hospital rounds.

"What's that student doctor doing talking to the patients? He's always stirring up trouble," said the doctor.

Nurse Shelley didn't comment.

"Keep him busy doing something else and make sure he stays away from my ward," he called after her as she walked through the door and into Reception.

Doctor Curr checked his watch. Good! Good! On time.

He walked back down the corridor past the wards, through an enclosed walk-way that separated the supply depot from the hospital, and into Mrs Kay's office.

"Good morning, Doctor," said Mrs Kay, the Supply Manager.

"Good morning, Mrs Kay," said the doctor, flicking through his keys. "Those aboriginals behaving themselves in the store?"

"Yes sir. It's only the ones that turn up drunk that cause any trouble."

You know where to send them," said the doctor, without looking at her.

He reached for the double doors of the cabinet above him.

"Damn keys!" he whispered. After three tries, he finally got the doors open.

He took out a large unmarked bottle and put it on the bench below the cabinet.

It took only minutes to change the full bottle for the empty. The doctor laughed quietly as the liquid slowly disappeared into the huge pipe that fed the drinking-water supply of the whole compound.

"Fluoride, my eye," he smirked.

"Yes Doctor? Did you say something?" called Mrs Kay.

"I don't know," he answered, "not only do I have to run a hospital, but there's all these other managerial jobs, as well! Talk about economy drives ."

"Sorry, can't hear you," called out Mrs Kay.

"Forget it."

What would you think if you really knew what was going into the aborigine's water everyday? Hey, Mrs Kay? He chuckled to himself.

The doctor could picture the sterilization-infertility drug slowly spreading throughout the water supply.

As he replaced the empty bottle and relocked the cabinet, he said:

"Supplies alright?"

"Yes Doctor."

Doctor Curr walked back past the wards, through the hospital, and out the other end, into another enclosed walkway joining the prison to the hospital.

He waited for the security door to be opened. Yes, he thought, on-schedule for golf and those tablets sure are working.

The metal door opened.

"Good morning Doctor," said the prison manager.

"Good morning Tom."

"Bad news today, I'm afraid, sir." Tom Martin pointed towards the prison cells, keys jangling in his hand.

He walked off with Doctor Curr following silently behind.

"Got a new one in this morning, Doctor," said Tom.

"Hmm," Doctor Curr looked at the prisoner through the bars.

"He goes by the name of Mop Thompson," laughed Tom. "You can see why." He pointed to the great mass of black curly hair on the prisoner's head.

The doctor didn't see anything funny about that.

"Young bloke here killed his girlfriend, sir," said Tom in a more serious tone.

"Tom, I don't see a problem here."

"This young bloke is one of the opinion leaders," explained Tom. "He also likes to stir up trouble in the compound, and it's a wonder he isn't a regular visitor in the prison."

The doctor looked at the prisoner.

The prison manager continued:

"This time he has gone too far. Wouldn't like to think what he'd try next."

Doctor Curr didn't waste any time on what course of action to take.

"Straight up to the ECT room with this one, Tom. I've got just the right kind of therapy for this type of criminal."

Doctor Curr walked on ahead. He looked at his watch. I can still make the tee-off in time, he thought.

Mop Thompson could be heard all through the prison. He screamed and kicked at the guards as they dragged him off towards the psychiatric wing of the hospital.

CHAPTER THREE

The morning sun streamed through the window. Alma had tossed and turned all night. She lay in bed, listening to the familiar voices coming from the kitchen.

Since reading more of the old book, many questions sprung to mind. What are they teaching the kids at the government-run school in the compound? It is supposed to be Aboriginal History, but it is far from the truth.

What food our ancestors gathered from the bush, or where they supposedly migrated from, are interesting pieces of information but no-where near the full picture.

Our people were deeply spiritual, just like this old book says.

Everything revolved around ancestral spirit-beings that lived in the spirit world. Also, daily spiritual activities were important to the people of the physical world.

One thing that had always stuck in her mind, even before reading the old book, was something Old Shirley had told her about telepathy. Before the White Man had come, the Aboriginal people could communicate across hundreds of miles by thought-power alone. Old Shirley had also said that after the White Man re-educated the 'native', telepathy had become a lost and forgotten skill.

During the night, pictures had flashed through her mind. She wasn't sure if the mental images had been dreams, or whether they were her real thoughts about past lives.

She tried to recall some of them.

A spirit entering a new-born baby. An old white man lying on a couch with a book resting on his chest. He looked like he was dead. How did she know he had died? He could've been sleeping. Well, she argued with herself, she just knew that he had died. And, he had died in his sleep!

Another question hit her. Could she have been that old white man in a past life? According to that old book, it was definitely possible. No! Couldn't be! How could it be?

She gave up. Too many questions and not enough answers. Alma decided to put all the figure-figure on hold, till she had read more of the old book.

"Alma!" shouted her mother. "Breakfast!"

"Coming." Alma felt sluggish from lack of sleep, but eventually got dressed in her favourite clothes - tight blue jeans, dark blue t-shirt and sandals - before going for breakfast.

Aunt Wendy sat at the kitchen table with Alma's parents. She didn't look too good. She would have a few more scars to add to the old ones.

Alma gave her a smile.

Aunt Wendy smiled back, then continued staring into her cup.

The wash-bucket was empty. Alma took it out to the front yard and filled it. She put her head under the lovely cool water. Her neck muscles tingled. She shook her long black hair, then wrapped her lips around the tap and drank to her heart's content. Hmm. Lovely cool water.

Today was going to be busy, she thought.

The heat from the morning sun warmed her wet hair.

Alma went back inside and rushed through breakfast, then went out to the front yard again and stood there for some time, wondering which direction she would go in.

"Alma, you forgot your lunch," yelled her mother from inside.

"Oh oh," she whispered as she walked back inside the shack.

"I'm not going to work today, Mum."

"Why not?"

"Got the sack."

"What happened?"

"He said I didn't work fast enough."

Alma could see the disappointment in her mother's eyes. One daughter left. Rosie and Faith already in the cemetery by the time Alma had reached the age of six. She had been lucky to survive whatever illness it was that had taken them. Her mother wanted her to have some sort of career, instead of ending up like most of the other children in the compound.

"That white fella didn't try anything on with you, did he love?" said her father, now sitting at the kitchen table.

"No, Dad," said Alma. "It was boring, anyway. I wanted to leave. He just speeded things up for me."

"Maybe you could get a job with the Aboriginal Council, in the office," said Aunt Wendy.

Dulcy and Frank looked at Aunt Wendy. All four burst out laughing.

"I'd rather she lose a leg than go work for the council," her father laughed. "White fellas with black skin - that lot!"

He took a spoonful of oatmeal and continued:

"Anyway, everyone knows that you have to be kin before you get into a job with the council. You can always come and work with your dear old dad, in the veggie patch."

"Thanks dad," smiled Alma.

"Well, I'm off to work," said her father.

" I've got to go see someone.   Be back later today mum."

She decided to go back and have another go at getting Old Shirley to talk about things.

Even at this early hour, the heat waves were shimmering on the track ahead of her.

Still, it wasn't too early for the flies. They clung to her body again and again, no matter how many times she swiped at them.

Alma smiled. No more emu eggs. She pictured a poor old mother emu racing about frantically in search for her eggs. How many eggs were taken over the years? She wondered where it was all heading - all this greed.

Old Shirley's shack was just ahead.

"Well! Hello," smiled the old woman. "I didn't think I'd be seeing you for quite awhile."

Alma joined her on the blanket under the gum tree, in front of her house.

The old red supply truck rounded the corner, delivered a few crates up ahead, and then stopped in front of Old Shirley's shack.

"There you go, old girl." A young man smiled as he put the crate of weekly supplies inside the shack.

"I'll give you 'old girl', you young scallywag." Old Shirley pointed the finger at him.

"And how are you today Alma?"

"Hi Joe," she smiled, then looked at the blanket to break the communication.

The truck continued on down the road.

"He's a nice boy that Joe," Old Shirley chuckled.

Alma laughed at the old woman's insinuation.

"Go grab yourself a cuppa - the billy's just been boiled."

Alma came back quickly. She was eager to get the old woman to talk.

"Tell me more about what it's like outside the compound. They teach you very little in the school and most of it is out-of-date, anyway."

"Look, love. You're heading for trouble with all this talk about outside."

Alma began to think twice about coming to see the old woman. But she tried again, anyway.

"I just want to have a look outside before I settle down. What's wrong with that? It's easy for you. You got the chance to see everything before they put up the electric fences."

Old Shirley looked at her for some time before replying.

"What year is it now?"

"2102." Alma felt the old woman weakening, knowing she loved to talk about the past.

"Well, it must've been fifty years ago when the electric fences went up. Before the compound officially became Australwitz One, we had a sort of camp here. Same with the other compound over at Sacred Rock.

"Some say that the government fenced us in because they were planning to wipe us out as a race. I don't know if that's true or not. But it sure is strange that hardly any babies get born these days. Surely they wouldn't go as far as that?"

Alma felt relief. She remained dead quiet now that the old woman finally started talking.

"The government said the fences were put up to protect us. There was some talk going around that a lot of Whites were angry about all the land repossession and money handouts."

Old Shirley finished her cuppa and went on:

"The government made a law, and at the time, everybody agreed to stick to it. That was fifty years ago. The Blacks stay on their land and the Whites stay on their land - no travelling across boundaries. Before that, things were free and easy. The Aboriginal Council was set up to run the affairs of the compound - they being the only ones allowed outside, mind you! - but we all know about them, don't we!"

Old Shirley slipped off into a sort of daydream for some minutes, then continued:

"There is something strange going on, though. If anyone gets caught outside the compound, they end up in the hospital prison. When they come back into the compound, the poor souls are like lost children. Zombies! Life has been wiped from their eyes. I don't usually talk about this because it only leads to trouble.

"The trees have ears. But I'm telling you, love, because you're only seventeen and I don't want to see you end up a zombie. Forget all this silly talk about going outside.

"There is plenty of free country over past the main canal - out beyond the veggie patches. Go walkabout over there when you get fidgety."

Alma lowered her head.

"You've seen the outside, Shirley."

She looked up and pleaded:

"I haven't been outside, ever!"

She then put her cup down on the blanket and leant forward.

"I've seen pictures in books. There is so much to see out there. We're no better than animals locked up in a zoo."

"I just don't want to see you get hurt, love. That's all."

Alma didn't budge.

Old Shirley looked at her pleading eyes, smiled and gave in.

"Well, who can blame you. I'd probably feel the same if I was in your spot. It's only natural I suppose. I can still remember the good old days. Dances, fast cars, train rides and plenty of travelling. You know, most Blacks and Whites mixed together back in those days without a care in the world. I think it was just a few greedy no-hopers that started all this business."

"How am I going to get out?" Alma thought aloud.

"I honestly don't know, love."

"What about all this talk of rebels that are supposed to live on the outside. Is it true? Aren't there stories about raids on the compounds? Or is it all just one big story to keep everyone from being bored to death?"

Old Shirley looked at Alma, then studied the ants crawling all over her cup. She looked straight up to search for what was making the racket in the tree above them. A big white cockatoo scraped his beak on the branch.

Finally, she answered Alma:

"There is an old man, even older than me - believe it or not - that lives in this compound, over on the west side. Go and see him."

*

Alma walked along the dirt track over towards the west side. She crossed the little bridges spanning the small waterways that lead off the main canal.

The sun was high up now. It was really hot, yet, some boys played football in the middle of the road.

She crossed the last waterway and an urgency rose up inside her. Could she really find a way out? It seemed hopeless but she just had to try.

There it was! She could see the big gum tree that Old Shirley had told her to look out for.

The old tin shack didn't look anything out of the ordinary, even though she could detect a strange sensation creep up on her as she approached it.

She tapped on the tin wall.

"Anyone home?" She waited in silence.

Then she could hear faint sounds coming from behind the shack. As she rounded the corner, children's voices could be heard.

An old man sat next to a fire in the middle of the yard. That must be Old Lloyd, she thought.

Young boys, five years old or so, were practising throwing spears and boomerangs. There was a garden patch further on down.

The old man turned a burning tree root in the fire, carefully inspecting it.

"Hi," said Alma.

The old man turned to look. Smoke, from a pipe in his mouth, drifted up in front of his face. He grunted, looked her up and down, and then went back to turning the tree root in the fire.

"Who do you belong to?" he finally said.

"I'm Alma Morgan. Frank Morgan is my father."

"Henry Morgan's tribe?"

"Yes, he was my grandfather."

"Hmm," grunted the old man, in approval. "One of the best sheepshearers there ever was."

"Yes. Dad told me a lot about him."

Old Lloyd took the tree root out of the fire, carefully inspected it and put it down to the side.

"What's that for?" said Alma. She pointed to the smouldering root.

"Boomerang."

Alma nodded.

"Well?" Old Lloyd said.

Alma thought that there would be no point in beating about the bush, so she just came straight out with it.

"I want to get out of this place. I was hoping you might help me."

The old man's eyes darted around the yard. He then gave Alma a long hard look before barking out an order to the boys.

"Take that gear over to the other side of the main canal. I'll be over soon. And don't lose that stuff in the water."

The young boys gathered up spears, boomerangs, other bits and pieces, and disappeared.

"Come inside," said Old Lloyd.

Alma followed the old man into the tin shack.

It consisted of one main room - in it were two chairs, a bed and a small table.

They sat down and he began talking in a hushed voice.

"What makes you think I can help?"

Alma explained how it was that she ended up coming to see him.

The old man listened without interrupting. Alma studied his aged face in the dark room. It showed signs of hardship with many scars and wrinkles. The eyes were quick, though - eyes with no fear. They were just like her father's eyes.

"If you have one drop of your grandfather's blood in you, I think it is safe to trust you," said Old Lloyd. "Alright, I'll help you. But just remember, this will be very dangerous. You might not even make it. There is a group of our people out there, and we send the odd handpicked boys and girls out to join them after some training, but you will have to go on your own.

"I can't let this get mixed up with our regular run. Do you understand?"

Alma nodded. She could barely control the rising emotions.

Old Lloyd told her what she must do.

He stopped abruptly, looking sharply at the side wall. Alma also heard the faint noise outside.

"You better go now," whispered the old man. "Here, take this." He handed her the old shoe box. She didn't look inside, as he had already told her what she needed to know about the journey.

Alma left the old man sitting in the dark.

CHAPTER FOUR

A couple of minutes before Alma left Old Lloyd's shack, a man ran from the side of the building, across the dirt track and up over the canal bank, to join another man.

He flopped down and rolled over onto his back, puffing and panting, while he recovered from the thirty-yard dash.

"Well?" Loo waited impatiently.

Fish held the side of his ribs. "Wait till I get my breath back."

"Look!" whispered Loo.

They watched a young woman leave Old Lloyd's place. She walked back the same way she had come - over to the east side.

A short time later Old Lloyd appeared in the doorway of his shack, scanned the area and after some time eventually walked off towards the main canal, up to the north.

"Well?" repeated Loo.

"I couldn't hear anything - they were too quiet," said Fish still puffing slightly.

"Something is going on," whispered Loo. "I can smell it."

"I've seen that girl before," said Fish. "She works in the tourism shop."

"What's her name?"

"Don't know." Fish shook his head slowly, at a loss.

"Forget Old Lloyd tonight. We'll follow her."

"What about Doctor Curr? He won't be too happy if we miss something." Fish adjusted the worn-out leather hat on top of his head. Perspiration poured down the sides of his face.

Loo thumped his fist into the dry grass that covered the canal bank.

He sat up and turned to face Fish, but the little man had leant down and was now soaking his head in the cool water of the canal.

"I don't care about Curr. Look! It doesn't matter how we catch them, just as long as we catch them."

"Yes, but Loo, what if it's a trick? They've caught us out before."

"Look, idiot. We've been watching that old goat for over a month this time round, and for what? Nothing. That's what."

Fish pleaded.

"I don't know - I don't want any trouble with that crazy doctor. Let's just follow the old man, like he told us to."

Smack! The back of Loo's big black hand hit Fish fair on the nose. Fish tried to blink away the tears that instantly blurred his vision.

"What did you do that for?"

"Idiot!" Loo stood up. "Get on your feet. Come on!"

Fish wiped his watery eyes and followed.

It was approaching evening by the time the girl had finally led them to the place where she must live. The sky was beginning to turn red in some parts. The sun headed for the horizon.

"That's Morgan's house," said Fish. " He's got crops in, over the other side of the big canal."

"She must be his daughter," whispered Loo. "You stay here and watch the place. I'll go and get us some tucker."

Fish watched the shack get darker and darker. He began to lose concentration and his stomach rumbled. He cursed Loo. Bet he's home feeding his face while I'm stuck here. Always the knucklehead left to do the dirty work.

Maybe this was a waste of time, and nothing would happen. Maybe it was a trick to lure them away. Right this minute, the rebels are probably breaking-in to the compound somewhere.

Fish thought about that new double-barrelled shotgun that he wanted. The only way he could get his hands on something like that would be to catch those rebels in the act. Then they would be able to collect the bonus promised to them by Doctor Curr.

Fish snapped alert at the sound of footprints behind him. Loo threw him a paper bag. He opened it and didn't waste any time throwing the food into his mouth.

"Well?"

"Nothing," mumbled Fish, mouth full.

"I'll go around the back and keep watch," whispered Loo. "Don't go to sleep."

Fish waited and waited. Still nothing. His eyelids wouldn't stay open. His head continually nodded forward and he found it hard to control it. Lying on his stomach helped a little.

Just as he had gotten his chin comfortably rested on the backs of his hands, there came sounds of footsteps.

"Come on!" whispered big Loo. "She's just gone out the back. Quick!"

In the darkness, Fish followed the vague outline in front of him. As Loo stopped to say something, Fish - half asleep - stumbled into the back of him.

"Damn idiot!" Loo held up a fist, but luckily for Fish, his mind seemed to be out ahead of them, in the darkness.

"She's headed for the main canal," Loo whispered.

Fish peered into the darkness. He could barely make out the figure way off in the distance. She was wearing a white top of some sort. Anybody with half a brain would know that you don't wear white at night, especially if you were trying to escape attention. So, maybe she wasn't up to no good. Maybe Loo made a mistake, and they were now barking up the wrong tree. Anyway, this sure was easy tracking, he thought.

On the whole, her direction seemed to be generally north, with the odd turn here and there. That would take her out to the unpopulated desert part of the compound.

It was obvious, now, that the girl wanted to go to the electric-fence boundary in a deserted part of the compound.

Fish followed along silently behind Loo.

What is she up to? he thought. How do the rebels sneak in and out? Maybe tonight they would find out. Then they could collect their big bonus.

A mental picture of a gleaming double-barrelled shotgun lay in front of Fish's eyes.

They tracked the girl to the electric fence. Then, like a ghost, she just disappeared! Fish stalked the area in ever widening circles while Loo studied the electric fence for an escape hole or something.

Fifteen foot high fence - no going over it or under it.

Then both men stood at the wire fence, gazing out into the darkness.

Fish realised that they had fallen for another old trick. The easy-to-follow white shirt. Once your eyes became used to the white shirt as the goal, the goal then changes to no more white shirt. And before the trackers are onto the trick, it's too late. But of course he wasn't about to bring it up with Loo – his nose still felt a little tender from the last time he tried to contribute some information. And Loo would have some explaining to do, especially as he took the honour of best tracker in the compound. Maybe he felt the tiredness more than Fish.

Loo leant forward and whispered:

"You go south - follow the fence back down to the main canal. I'll follow it up the other way. If you find her, follow her. If you find the rebels, don't try anything, just come and get me. If you don't find anything, forget about it, and go back to Old Lloyd's shack and watch him. I'll see you in front of the supply shed in the morning."

Fish started out cautiously but soon tired of the detective work and dawdled the rest of the way back to the canal. No sign of the girl or the rebels. He reached the wide canal, sat down and threw stones into the water for awhile.

Maybe she just headed out to meet the boyfriend - happens often enough. Maybe she is already back at home, asleep in bed. Maybe Loo found her and headed back.

The tiredness really had a hold of Fish now. No good sitting out here, he thought. Fish headed for his bed.

*

Alma sat on the hot sand. She looked up through the leaves of the stunted tree. The sun poured heat down upon her. It had been a long walk – all night and all day. Time for a good rest, and a good sleep.

She thought back to the beginning of the previous night.

She hoped her parents would have understood when they found the letter on her bed this morning.

The strange slippers were still on her feet. Old Lloyd had put them in the shoe box and told her to wear them until now. They had been made from small emu feathers, tied together with strands of human hair. She realised that it would be difficult to track her while wearing these.

A feeling of joy crept up inside her as she recalled her escape from the compound last night. Tiredness mixed with joy. She closed her eyes and retraced her steps the night before, hoping to have followed Old Lloyd's orders and not slipped up.

It had been so simple! How could the compound guards not think of it? Old Lloyd had told her that the water would be deep but she had managed quite easily. The electric fence ran across the top of the main canal, but naturally electricity couldn't be allowed to go anywhere near the water.

Therefore the bottom fence, that the water passed through, couldn't be electrified.

Alma had no problems with the small wire door - made by the rebels - in the bottom fence on the canal floor. Holding her breath for so long had frightened her, but she resurfaced on the other side with a gasp for air and a smile.

She had then followed the main canal out into the desert until morning.

Old Lloyd had told her to leave the canal and walk into the desert – keeping the sun on the back of her neck, just behind her right ear. At noon she had slept for some hours before continuing on, with the sun blaring into her eyes from the left.

Alma adjusted her canvas bag to make a pillow and prepared for a long sleep. With luck she would reach the rebel's camp in about three days.

She snuggled into the rough pillow and a deep sleep overcame her.

In what appeared to be no time at all, she found herself opening her eyes to the chatter of two small birds in the branches above her. Bright pink clouds hid the morning sun far off on the eastern horizon.

Not long after, she felt the first rays of the huge fireball as it rose above the cloudy horizon.

Alma smiled. Freedom! No more compound. No electric fences.

After eating, and a good long drink, she headed further into the desert.

There were no landmarks. There was no map. The sun was her only guide. The land lay flat as far as the eye could see.

Occasionally, dwarfed trees broke the monotony.

By the time the sun had reached the top of the sky, Alma had found a bigger tree with a little more shade than the others.

She lay down to rest from the midday heat but soon became aware of a peculiar buzzing sound. It came closer.

An aeroplane!

After some minutes the plane disappeared and the desert fell silent once more. She hoped the speckled shade of the tree had camouflaged her from the pilot. She rested for awhile and then walked on.

By the time the sun had sunk behind the far-off horizon, Alma dropped, exhausted. It had been a long hot day. She definitely wasn't used to this and wondered whether she would survive the trip.

The idea of eating something never even crossed her mind. She lay under a tree and went to sleep.

Two more days passed. No more aeroplanes - only goannas, smaller lizards, snakes, birds, and lots of hot red sand.

She wondered how the rebels survived in this barren land. No water, anywhere! Lucky I have plenty of water, she thought.

Four days had passed and still no sign of the rebels. Alma started to get anxious. A feeling of loneliness overcame her.

She stared at the precious few mouthfuls of water left in her last plastic bottle.

According to Old Lloyd someone should've found her by the end of the third day. She felt as if she was the only person in the whole wide world.

The stars came out above. She began to feel so small and insignificant compared to the boundless space up above.

The last of the water tasted terrible. It tasted like the wine she had tried when she was a child - done as a dare.

Alma hadn't touched alcohol since. Other kids laughed at her, poked fun and teased her all the way through her teen years, but she had held fast.

She could even see their faces now, laughing and looking at her as if she was some kind of a weirdo.

She didn't care what they thought of her.

No water!

Alma pulled the biscuits out of the bag. The last of the food! She ate half the packet. A big mistake. Now she felt even thirstier.

"Where are you? Where are the desert people?" she yelled.

The desert replied with silence. She looked at all the hot burnt sand - it was endless.

Alma couldn't sleep that night. The dryness in her mouth tortured her and the emptiness in her stomach continually niggled at her.

In the morning she ate the rest of the biscuits.

Her feet were blistered.

"This is it!" she told herself. "No more. I've had enough!"

Old Lloyd had told her to just keep walking and the rebels would pick her up. Damn him! It must be at least five days now – he had said three!

She stayed in the shade of the tree.

No more, thought Alma. She just couldn't go on anymore.

By nightfall she was cursing herself.

You silly stupid girl. Who do you think you are? You are nothing. A nobody. Too smart for your own good. Yes! That's your problem.

A long forgotten sensation rose up inside her chest. Her throat tightened. She couldn't hold it back. The tears streamed down her cheeks and into the corners of her mouth. She licked at the salty taste.

Alma threw her arms to the ground and buried her face in the hot sand – she cried her heart out.

The next day she wriggled and rolled on the ground in terrible pain. The night had been full of horrible nightmares – death, murder, demons, someone chasing her, someone cutting into her arms and legs.

As the sun came up she suddenly realised that all sense of time had disappeared. Occasionally she opened her eyes, only to quickly shut them as the red hot rays shot into her very soul.

She helplessly murmured for someone to come.

By nightfall her body had gone completely numb. There was no feeling or sensation at all.

Mostly, she just dreamed.

Soon it was hard to tell which was reality and which was dream.

If she hid in the black box, the devils and murderers couldn't get her. But then they would find a way in. Someone opened the lid of the black box. She pretended to lie there as if she was dead.

The demons left her alone when they thought she was dead. They would laugh at her and then close the lid.

That was the safest way to handle it.

But then the demons kept coming back and opening the lid. They knew she was pretending. They stuck spears into her body, laughed at her and tickled her.

She couldn't hide.

A demon opened the lid of the black box again. He slid his hand under her head and lifted it slightly. She opened her eyes. He had a large knife! Alma could feel the blade cutting into her throat. The demon laughed at her again. "You are mine now," he sneered.

Alma could feel a rage building up inside her body. She somehow knew that if the demon could cut her throat he would take her head away and carry it around on his belt for the rest of eternity. Her head! Hanging and dangling from his belt! No! Never! She screamed.

She gathered up all the strength and reached out to grab the demon's throat but he was too quick and managed to evade her.

She reached up further still, clawing at his eyes. Harder and harder she fought. Her fingernails went deeper and deeper into those terrible yellow and blood-red eyes.

Blood poured out of the demon's eye-sockets.

The evil spirit showed signs of weakening. He backed away. Alma pulled him closer, with fingers hooked into his eyes.

He screamed.

She dug her fingers in harder. Gritting her teeth, eyes screwed tight, she tried with all her might.

"There, there. It's alright. You're safe now," came a soft voice.

"Mum, is that you?" Alma cried as she opened her eyes.

An emu stared down at her. Alma squinted her eyes in disbelief. An emu?

The emu smiled at her.

"You will be alright now."

Alma relaxed, pulling back her outstretched hands. She felt secure, lying in the black box, now that the emu was there to look after her.

The emu had saved her!

A sense that something peculiar was about to happen took hold of her. Suddenly, a surge of energy shot up through her body and into her head. The exhilarating sensation moved up to the top of her skull, and seemed to slowly build up in pressure, where it finally exploded out of the top of her head.

She felt at peace and drifted off to sleep.

After some time a thought occurred to her. She panicked.

"How long have I been asleep?" she asked out loud. "Where has the emu gone? It hasn't left me, has it? I don't want that evil demon to come back.

"Emu! Come back! Where are you?" she called out. As she opened her eyes she lifted her head to see better.

Someone was holding her hand. She pulled back without thinking.

A black face, covered in an even blacker bushy beard, peered down at her. Bright white teeth filled a broad smiling face.

Alma gave up. She didn't know what to make of it. Was she still dreaming or not?

At least it felt like the evil spirit had gone.

Slowly she closed her eyes, with the strange thought that everything would be alright now.

No more dreams. Just sleep.

CHAPTER   FIVE

Loo paced back and forth outside the supply shed. The morning sun pelted down the heat. Fish was an hour late.

Just as Loo decided to go find him, Fish walked around the corner.

His walk was unsteady and he rubbed the back of his neck.

Loo waited till he got right up close.

Bang!

Fish landed on the seat of his pants.

"What was that for?" he said.

"Get up!" yelled Loo. "Any sign of that girl?"

"Nothing. She just disappeared, Loo."

"Come on," said Loo. "We'll go and see the doctor."

Fish followed Loo over to the back door of the compound hospital.

Doctor Curr appeared at the door some minutes later.

"What is it?"

"Young girl," explained Loo. "Seventeen or so. Morgan. She was at Old Lloyd's place yesterday. We tracked her to the fence on the northwest side, last night. Just disappeared. No tracks this morning. Be the work of those rebels from the desert, I'd say."

"Look here, you two. I pay you extra for information and captures. I repeat! Captures! So far you haven't brought one of those rats in. I want some captures! How else can I interrogate them to find the whereabouts of the secret hide-out?

"If you don't start getting some products, you just might find out what it's like to be in a prison. Get it?"

Doctor Curr looked at Loo, then at Fish.

"Wait here." He disappeared back into the compound hospital. Shortly he returned with a letter. He handed it to Loo.

"This is an authorisation for supplies from Mrs Kay at the supply depot. It also gets you three horses from the Aboriginal Council stables. I don't care how long it takes but you better bring back someone. Or else!"

Doctor Curr turned to leave but then suddenly paused on his way back into the hospital.

"I'll have a plane from Broken Hill sent out to search the area. They might be lucky and spot the girl. We won't get any further help from outside. Do you understand? The government thinks that these rebels are a figment of our imagination. I want some results!"

Loo and Fish watched the little doctor disappear back into the white building.

Loo then smiled at the letter in his hand. He realised a winner when he saw one. This letter gave them a pass for a good long walkabout. Who cares if they get someone or not. Well, it would be an added bonus if they happened to stumble onto one of those rebels. And the worst would be a short stint in prison if they failed. He laughed off the threat from the little white man in his funny little white coat.

He signalled Fish to follow him to the supply shed.

Mrs Kay read the letter, shaking her head in disapproval.

Loo was already throwing things into sacks.

Suddenly he stopped cold. Fish also stopped, to watch him.

Loo looked at the north wall and out through the barred window.

"What?" said Fish.

"You get the rest of the stuff. I'll be back in one hour. Don't forget some tucker for the horses. Meet you at the stables out front."

"Where are you going?" pleaded Fish.

Loo didn't answer.

He grabbed an old delivery van from the supply depot garage. A trail of dust hung in the hot air behind him as he headed north, over the main canal, and out to the electric fence.

He had been out earlier that morning, before Fish arrived at the supply depot, and searched the same ground he had covered the previous night. This time he decided to search in the south, toward the main canal, where Fish had gone the night before.

Sure enough! Her boot-tracks vanished into thin air, right next to the fence.

He looked at the top of the fence. An image flashed through his mind of the girl jumping over the electrified fence? No way!

He looked down the line of the fence - as straight as a gun barrel.

Loo didn't know why but this time he had a hunch about which the way the girl went.

The desert sand got a thorough going over as he walked slowly along the fence line, toward the main canal.

Nothing! Almost half way to the canal, and not a sign. A dozen times now the thought had entered his mind to turn back. It was useless.

He was an experienced tracker and there definitely was no sign of the girl's tracks.

Then something caught his eye.

A small feather?

A small emu feather! Strange to see an emu feather in this compound, he thought. All hunted out years ago.

Could've blown in, but highly unlikely - considering how far the Whitey had to go to find emu eggs these days.

Loo tickled his lips with the feather while he stared out through the fence into the desert. Wind could've blown it in.

He looked at the small feather once more. What's this? He brought the feather up closer to his eyes.

A hair? A small thin piece of hair was twisted around the feather. He pulled it away from the feather, and compared it to one of his own.

They near enough matched. It must be a human hair.

Loo thought hard.

Emu feathers and human hairs?

It rings a bell. Now, where had he come across this strange combination before?

A cold shiver crept up the back of his neck and tingled the top of his scalp.

Black magic!

Shoes made out of emu feathers and human hair. He had heard stories as a child. Ghost stories about evil spirits coming to get bad boys. Evil spirits that would wear strange slippers made from feathers and hair.

Murder, sorcery and all that type of stuff the old people used to try to scare the kids with.

His head started to hurt. The headache prevented him from recalling anymore of the long forgotten memories.

Loo walked on towards the canal.

He occasionally checked the fence for holes, but his attention was now drawn towards the water.

Soon, he stood on the massive bank and looked down at the great body of water slowly drifting along out under the fifteen foot high fence.

The slowly moving water had a calming effect on him. He felt the coolness in the surrounding air.

As he continued to stare at the water flowing through the wire mesh fence, he whispered out loud.

"How do they get in and out?"

The shadows of the wire danced about on the moving surface of the water.

He followed the lines of the wire mesh down into the clear water while he tried to figure out the riddle.

"How do they get in and out?" he repeated.

Loo looked out through the fence and followed the winding canal as it made its way out into the desert and back towards the town of Broken Hill.

He looked at the wire mesh again.

Water! That's it! The bottom half of the fence has no electricity running through it!

What an idiot. He gave himself a clout across the top of his head with his leather hat.

Within five minutes Loo had discovered the small wire-mesh trapdoor cut into the fence at the bottom of the canal.

By the time he walked back to the van, up along the electric fence, his clothes were already dry.

The old van sped over the dry dusty track.

Loo punched at the front of the windscreen. "We're in business!"

He headed for the stables.

CHAPTER   SIX

Alma could hear strange noises. Mumbled sounds and echoes raised her out of a deep sleep. Rocks were being struck. She could hear the crackle of a fire.

On opening her eyes, she looked straight up. Vague shadows flickered high up on a rock ceiling.

A cave?

The roof was so high, the light from the fire almost didn't reach it.

She glanced from side to side without moving her head. The fire flared at her from the left. A dark figure sat on the ground to her right.

Was she still dreaming?

The heat from the flames felt real enough. Was she dead? Was this the hell that the white teachers spoke of? Were they right? Was it true?

Slowly she lifted her head. Fear took hold. She wanted to run like a mad woman.

A hand came down over her face before she could move. It stroked her forehead.

Alma looked past the hand to find a smiling face.

"Water?" said a girl about the same age as herself.

Alma nodded, still puzzled.

The water tasted so good.

"What is this place? Where am I?" whispered Alma.

"This is the Hidden Valley," said the smiling girl. "It's our home."

She then waved to someone.

Two men walked over from another fire a short distance away.

The older man squatted next to Alma.

"What's your name?"

"Alma Morgan. Where am I?"

The old man looked around the vast cavern.

"This is an underground cave. It's one of many linked together by an underground river."

He pointed to a far wall. Alma could see the water flowing slowly by. Her gaze shifted in all directions, trying to take in the huge and vast dark space. She felt so small.

"Morgan, you say?" said the old man, stroking his grey beard. "Ever heard of Henry Morgan?"

"He was my grandfather. Frank Morgan is my father," said Alma.

"Old Henry was the quickest sheepshearer there was, you know?" smiled the old man.

"Yes, that's what my father says too."

The old man looked into the fire, still stroking his beard.

"Get some rest," he finally mumbled. "Liddy will take good care of you." He pointed to the girl sitting beside her.

Liddy smiled, then offered more water.

Alma gladly accepted.

The two men walked off into the darkness.

Alma drank some more water. She tried to stay awake but her eyelids wouldn't stay open. The warmth from the fire felt friendlier now, and she dozed off.

When Alma woke again, the cave was still there. How long had she been here? There was no way of knowing if it was night or day. The darkness only occasionally gave way to the camp fires dotted here and there across the cave floor.

Liddy told her that the old man was the leader of the tribe.

"His name is Old George," she said.

Alma slept another two long sleeps. Recovery came quick. Energy flowed back into her body, thanks to Liddy's special tea.

"Who was the man that found me out in the desert?" asked Alma.

"Nulla," smiled Liddy.

"Is he here? I'd like to thank him."

"He was the man standing next to Old George, when you first woke up. Remember?"

Alma nodded and tried to recall the image of his face.

"He will be back tomorrow. You can meet him then."

The following morning Alma sat eating breakfast with Liddy and a couple of the other girls.

A young man walked over from another campfire and joined them.

He squatted next to Alma. The girls giggled.

"You feeling better today?" he said with a smile.

"How do you know if it's daytime?" asked Alma, looking around the dark cave walls.

The young man laughed.

"You'll soon get the hang of it."

"I feel alright now, thanks to Liddy. You're Nulla - the one who found me in the desert, aren't you?"

Nulla nodded his head.

"How did you find me? I thought I was gone for sure."

"Old Lloyd, from the compound, came to your rescue. He's the one you really should be thanking."

Alma was confused. "How?"

"He sent a message through the spirit world," said Nulla.

Alma recalled what Old Shirley had told her about telepathy.

"You were funny," laughed Nulla.

Alma smiled. "What do you mean by that?"

"I tried to pick you up when you were lying out there in the desert, and all you wanted to do, was wring my neck and scratch out my eyes."

"I don't remember."

"Well, you did! Very strong grip, too. I nearly ended up in the dreamtime with my ancestors."

"All that I can remember is some terrible dream. Demons and emus talking to me. Oh! Now I remember your face. I knew it was a young man but now the picture is stronger. Yes. I can remember your big black bushy beard."

Both Alma and Nulla laughed as they looked at each other.

"No, really - thank you." Alma looked at him and stopped laughing.

"It's alright, but remember, save it for Old Lloyd when you run into him next time." It was Nulla's turn to be serious.

Alma nodded.

Nulla stood up and walked off. Alma watched him go.

A couple of the girls giggled some more, and Alma blushed but didn't know why.

Many days passed. The girls taught Alma how to find food, water and shelter in the desert. She didn't see Nulla but thought of him often.

Slowly she regained her strength. The food gathering trips in the desert were a daily occurrence now.

Liddy had told her about life in the caves. An underground river ran from east to west. There were so many caves linked together that the tribe of rebels hadn't travelled the full length yet. The caves just went on and on - following the river.

The rebels numbered a hundred or so. Only a few at a time made trips to the desert surface each day. Any planes or trackers would be less likely to discover them.

The first day Alma went out of the cave with Liddy, she was surprised when shown the secret entrance. It was similar to the escape route from the compound.

Liddy, Alma and another girl had walked along the side of the underground river to the end of the cave.

The water appeared to bubble up from under the cave wall. The girls waded into the shallow water, ducked under the surface and passed through a hole in the wall. Then resurfaced on the other side, into another smaller cave.

When Alma wiped the water from her eyes, she could see a bright light high up at the top of a steep slope. Daylight!

As she reached the top, she looked back down at the water on the floor of the cave. Amazing! It looked like a pool of water that had gathered in the deepest corner of the cave.

Up on top, the desert entrance to the cave was a crack in a huge flat rock. Small trees surrounded the rock. It would be very hard to spot from the air above - only just enough room for one person to squeeze through.

"Where's Nulla?" Alma asked Liddy while they gathered food. "I haven't seen him for days."

"He should be back tonight. They went hunting."

"Have they gone on a raid to the compound?" asked Alma.

"You don't miss much," Liddy laughed. "I don't like it when they go there." She added, on a more serious note.

"Were you born in the caves, Liddy?"

"Yes."

"So you've never seen the compound."

"No."

"It's not as bad as you might think, you know."

"Not for me thanks," Liddy shook her head at the mere thought of it.

"How long has the tribe lived in the caves?" asked Alma.

"I'm not sure, but Old George tells us stories about the old times.

She put her basket down and sat on the sand. Alma joined her. Then Liddy looked off into the distance for a spell before she began to tell Alma as much as she knew.

"Old George says they built the compound about two generations ago. Our people wandered all over the land before the white man came. Then they gave us the rights to settle in sacred areas. Old George says the Blacks controlled a quarter of all the land up till two generations ago. About then, the miners and land developers started to protest and said it was unfair. Old George says they were just being greedy."

Liddy inspected her basket for a moment. She picked some dead leaves off the berries and grass roots, and when satisfied, she continued:

"The Aboriginal Council agreed to the government plan to make two compounds. For safety, they put up the electric fences - to keep out any evil white people. That was what they were told, anyway. Old George says that the Aboriginal Council is no good - only the white man's puppets. He says most Whites are good people, just like most of our people. He says that most Whites understand our concerns and tradition, but for some unknown reason the government is trying to wipe out our race. That's why we have our people out here in the caves - in our Hidden Valley. But surely you know about all this?"

Alma shook her head in confusion. "I've heard stories. But I can't get to the bottom of it."

She bent forward and picked at some grass roots growing near her bare feet.

"Leave them, " said Liddy. "They give you a tummy ache."

"There is this terrible doctor that runs the compound," said Alma. "People that come back into the compound, after being in his hospital, tell strange stories. And some of them look really weird, like they have lost the will to live. That doctor gives them drugs that make them crazy."

"Nulla said he went into the hospital on a raid one time," said Liddy. "He says that the doctor is using our people in secret experiments. Something about torturing people with electricity."

Liddy seemed agitated, but continued after a moment.

"Look, Alma, I don't know if I really should be talking to you about this, but you have to find out sometime - especially if you have any plans about going back there to live."

Liddy stopped talking and ran her fingers through the burnt red sand.

"Well, go on - what?" Alma said.

"Well, there's talk going around, that some of the girls in the compound can't have children. They think that the government is using some kind of drug in the water supply. It couldn't be done any other way. It has to be done that way. Some women are so strong that the drug doesn't work on them yet, or, the drug is designed to sterilize them slowly - so they won't notice until it's too late. Anyway, you must've heard about this before. It can't be news to you."

Alma looked away from Liddy. She had heard some stories but just couldn't bring herself to believe that there would be such evil people living in the world capable of doing such a thing.

Liddy went on:

"That's why we live out here. It's not the only reason. There is also our belief in the Dreamtime. The white man is hell-bent on brainwashing our younger ones and they are succeeding. Just speak to any of the youngsters in there these days. Of course, you're different - you got out. But most of those poor souls in there are walking around in their sleep."

Alma didn't like what she had heard. Could she be sterile? If so, she would never have a normal life. Never! She suddenly felt worthless.

Liddy grabbed Alma's arm.

"That's why we steal children from the compound. Some of them are strong and survive the poison fed to them by the doctor. We have special herbs. Otherwise we would end up an inbred lot - no use to any one. The raids are risky but something has to be done before our whole civilization goes down the tube. Old George and the other elders have tried to tell the people in the compound but they just won't listen. The white scientists have tricked them into believing the old story about old cultures dying off to make way for new ones. The Aboriginal Council takes government handouts and closes their eyes to everything."

Alma looked into Liddy's eyes. She didn't want to believe it.

"No, it just can't be."

"It is!" Liddy held Alma's arm tighter.

That night, back in the cave, Alma sat silently by the campfire. She was lost in a world of her own.

A loud splash pulled her out of the despair. A man jumped up out of the underground river. He ran towards the elder's campfire. He yelled at them in a language that she couldn't understand.

Alma turned to Liddy:

"What's happening?"

"Sssh!" Liddy was listening to the young man.

After the commotion died down, she told Alma what was happening.

"Nulla and Fred have been caught." Tears welled up in Liddy's eyes.

"What? The compound?"

"Yes. Billy was the only one to escape. They didn't see him. But they got my Freddie."

After a heated discussion that Alma couldn't understand, four men and a boy gathered up spears and a small carry-bag and made their way out through the secret underwater doorway.

That night Alma couldn't sleep.

With plenty of time to have thought things over, she had come to the only solution. While everyone in the cave slept, Alma slipped out into the desert.

She had made up her mind to return to the compound. She just couldn't stay in the safety of the caves while her people were doomed to slowly rot to death. Even if she failed, at least it was worth the try. Maybe she could return Nulla's help. It all looked totally impossible from where she stood, but just to do nothing would be unbearable.

The desert stretched out before her. The sun was not up over the horizon yet.

Alma dreaded the thought of going off into the desert again by herself. Slowly, she walked off towards the south.

CHAPTER SEVEN

Nulla sat on the edge of a prison bed.

He held his head in his hands. The throbbing headache wouldn't stop. Every time he tried to recall the last few days, the pain shot through to his eyes.

He tried to force himself to remember.

One thing continually came up through the blackness of his mind.

An older man. He could see an older man in a white coat, standing in front of him. Something about going to Sydney for a conference, he had said. Something about not being able to treat this prisoner till he returned. Surely it wasn't a dream. Then there was something else - a bigger man appeared to be standing next to the smaller one, laughing.

Nulla closed his eyes.

He tried with all his might to remember what else happened.

A picture of fists and boots! He shied away from the memory. It hurt his head. Four men. That was it. It all came back now. Four prison guards beat the living daylights out of him. Then a nurse, or someone like that, jabbed a needle into his arm. Then he went unconscious.

Nulla let go of his head and rubbed the back of his of neck.

He felt dizzy.

All he wanted to do was lie down and go to sleep. But he knew that that was out of the question. Must think! He forced himself.

The Raid! We were on a raid.

Now the whole chain of events came flooding back more vividly.

His head lightened up as he recalled more and more.

Someone must've told them! Someone tipped them off. They knew where the secret entrance to the compound was, and they were waiting.

Who?

The only thing that had changed recently was that new girl they had found out in the desert. What was her name? Alma! She had come from the compound. It had to be her.

Nulla looked at the cell bars in front of him.

Freddie! He looked past the bars and across the corridor to where his friend lay in a separate cell.

"Freddie!" he whispered.

No answer.

Freddie slowly raised himself up on one elbow. He winced in pain.

"Where's Billy?" said Nulla, a little louder.

"Don't know," said Freddie. They both looked around the prison. Through the bars of the many cells they could see a dozen or so dejected souls. But no sign of Billy.

Either they had him somewhere else or he got away.

Rage took hold of Nulla. This is no better than an animal-cage. I've just got to get out of here! He felt the anger burning inside.

"How the hell are we going to get out of here?" said Freddie.

They stared through the bars at each other.

Two days went by.

The nerves were raw.

Freddie took to pacing up and down his eight-foot cell. He was beginning to lose it.

Nulla tried to calm him down but didn't get anywhere.

The big man with the evil laugh turned out to be the prison manager, Tom Martin.

Every day he would go through the same routine. Nulla just ignored the taunts, but other prisoners, from the compound, took it to heart.

On and on it went.

"Pull 'em down out of the trees, cut their tails off, teach 'em how to talk and they think they own the bloody joint.

"Bludgers wouldn't work in an iron lung.

"Hey! When you see the whites of their eyes... Shoot!

"Jacky, Jacky, he no fooly - he put white wash on his tooly."

On and on it went.

Six or seven days went by.

As usual, in the evenings, Nulla got a visit from the prison manager. And, as usual, he had his black baton with him. Tom Martin slapped the side of his leg with the baton.

"Alright, Blackie Jackie. This is your last chance. Come on - where are your mates hiding out?"

Nulla sat motionless on the edge of his prison bed. He knew what was coming, but couldn't do a damn thing about it.

Two guards stood on either side of the prison manager.

Tom Martin grabbed a hand full of Nulla's hair and yanked him to the concrete floor.

Nulla thought, what the hell - might as well get one in.

He kicked up into Tom Martin's groin. It was a weak attempt. His legs were already badly damaged from all the previous interrogations.

Tom Martin let out an agonised groan.

"Right! Blackie Jackie. You're done for, this time. I'll save Doctor Curr the trouble."

Nulla's head jerked back as the steel-capped boot connected. The back of his head slammed into the steel frame of the bed. Blackness fell in all around him with boots, fists and batons raining down from everywhere.

Sometime later Nulla tried to open his eyes. He couldn't - they were stuck together. He worked at his eyes for quite awhile with injured fingers. Eventually, he managed to pry one of them open.

He looked around the prison.

Silence.

The night guards were on duty. He must've been out cold for a long time.

Nulla could only move an inch or so before the pain became too much.

Sometime later, he woke again to the sound of voices.

"I've just arrived back from Sydney. Tell Tom to lay off. I'll sort this out myself. We'll get to the bottom of this tomorrow."

Nulla opened his half-good eye. It was the same little man in the white coat that he had briefly come across before, when first caught.

Anyway, who cares what they do to me now, he thought. I've had enough! I give up! They won't get anything out of a dead man. My body is beyond pain. Nulla fell into a deep sleep.

*

Darcy was in charge of the rescue party.

He had three other men and a boy with him. They stood in the dark shadows of the car-park and watched a little man, in a white coat, leave the main complex. He entered a nearby house and not long after the lights went out.

The hospital and prison lights remained on.

Outside the electric fence, next to the car-park, were a group of houses that belonged to the Aboriginal Council.

"Let's go have a look at the snot-noses," whispered Darcy. "Billy! You come with me. You lot, stay here."

Billy followed Darcy through the darkness, to the back of the Aboriginal Council houses.

Darcy pointed to a weak light coming from one of the houses. Both men peered through a lace curtain, into the kitchen. Three men sat at the kitchen table, playing cards and drinking beer.

After some time, Darcy's patience grew thin. We've waited too long, he thought. Time for action. He reached for the back door handle.

At the same instance, two of the card players stood up and walked to the back door.

Darcy and Billy back-pedalled and hid behind the water tank.

They watched the two men stagger off in different directions towards different houses.

Darcy pointed to one of the men.

"Is that Benny Lock?"

"Yeah! Looks like him," whispered Billy.

Before Benny Lock, a council elder, could turn around to close the door behind him, the point of a spear jabbed into his ribs. He froze solid.

"One sound and you're a dead man," whispered Darcy.

"Yeah! You black runt," added Billy.

"Into the front room, you fat pig," ordered Darcy.

When they got there, Darcy continued:

"Ring the hospital. Tell them that your boy is sick, and he needs a nurse to take a look at him. Tell them that he's got trouble breathing or something. You just want a nurse to take a quick look at him - no doctor, right?"

Darcy could see that the council elder was rotten drunk and couldn't be trusted. He flicked the spear at the elder's eye. Blood flowed from a cut above the eyebrow.

"Ah! What did you do that for?" said the council elder.

"No funny stuff if you want to see your family again," snapped Darcy.

Within minutes, Benny Lock and his boy stood at the front of the hospital door. Darcy and the others were close by, ready to pounce.

The night nurse opened the front door after recognising Benny Lock's voice on the security phone.

Darcy rushed the door. The others followed, bundling their captives into the main corridor.

By the time the rest had caught up with Darcy, he already had the bulky night guard pinned to his chair - spear pressed firmly into his flabby neck.

"On the floor fat boy," Darcy ordered. "You can join him, Lock."

Two of the raiding party stayed to guard them, while Darcy and Billy took the nurse into the reception area.

"I want the key that opens that door there," ordered Darcy. He pointed to the door leading to the prison section.

Once opened, he pushed the nurse along the enclosed walkway and up to the metal door of the prison.

"Open it!" demanded Darcy.

"I can't!" The nurse shook in fear. She began crying.

"Stop crying!" said Darcy. "Why can't you open it?"

"It has to be done from their side. We have to phone through from reception first and then they open it." She looked at her watch. " It's nearly time for their meal. I can ring them and say that they have to take it early because we have a staff shortage in the hospital."

Tears rolled down the nurse's face. Darcy figured she must be telling the truth.

She looks too scared to try any funny business. He pulled her back to the phone at the reception.

The nurse had just picked up the phone when she stopped cold. She looked past Darcy.

A hospital patient, dressed in the standard white full length gown, walked towards them.

"Nurse! I can't sleep."

The patient was totally oblivious to the fact that five rebels, dressed in no more than string belts around their wastes, held the hospital staff and others captive.

He ran his fingers through his long curly black hair.

Darcy summed him up in an instant - harmless and probably drugged-up to the hilt.

"Go back to bed, Jimmy," said the nurse. She tried to smile. "I'll bring something in a minute."

"I got nightmares again," mumbled Jimmy. As he turned and headed back to bed, he added: "It's those damn devils - just can't seem to get rid of them."

Jimmy shuffled along still talking to no-one in particular.

Darcy said to himself: "Probably didn't even see the spears pointed at the captives, or if he did, it definitely didn't register."

The nurse, with the phone still in her hand, pushed the button to connect the prison wing.

"Yes ...Your food is ready... I know... I have to attend to a patient... You'll have to take your meals early... I'm sorry, but the patients come first."

She sighed heavily as she put the phone down.

"They're coming for it now. Please don't hurt anyone."

Darcy and Billy raced into the enclosed walkway. They stood either side of the prison door.

The key turned from inside.

Slam!

The prison guard got hit in the face. He fell backwards.

Billy kicked him between the legs.

Darcy jumped over him and raced down the corridor.

Further down, another guard had just entered the corridor.

He reached for his pistol.

Darcy already had his throwing arm cocked.

He let the spear go, with full force.

The guard tried to jump to the side and fire at the same time.

"Ahhh!" The spear got him in the left arm. The right hand fired a shot.

Darcy followed the spear, at a full run.

The guard's attention went straight to the pain in his arm. It was only for a split second, but that was too long.

Darcy had already let his boomerang go.

Straight between the eyes!

The guard managed to fire a second shot. It hit the ceiling as he tumbled over backwards - out cold.

Darcy grabbed the keys and opened the cell door.

Nulla had managed to stand as best he could. They smiled at each other. Darcy took hold of his arm and helped him out.

Billy took the keys and opened all the cell doors.

"Let's get the hell out of here!" said Freddie.

Billy frowned at the ugly sight of his two friends.

"What the devil did they do to you?" He looked Nulla and Freddie up and down. Their faces were unrecognisable from the swellings and missing teeth. Blood-matted hair made it look even more ghastly.

Billy snarled: "Let's get that little ferret in the white coat and string him up."

"No! No!" said Nulla. "No killing! They'll have the whole damn army after us if we do anything stupid now. Leave it for another time. We know where to find all of them when the time comes."

"Yeah! Come on. Let's get out of here right now," said Darcy. "Someone will have heard those gun shots."

"One last thing, before we go," said Nulla. "It'll only take a couple of seconds."

The rest headed out into the car-park, while Nulla and Darcy checked the hospital beds.

"Is that Mop Thompson?" said Darcy.

"Hey! Mop! Is that you?" added Nulla.

Mop Thompson lay on his side in the hospital bed. He stared at the wall.

Darcy bent down to look into his eyes. "Mop! What's wrong?"

Mop didn't answer.

"The eyes are open but there isn't anyone home," continued Darcy. "He's nothing but one of those zombies!"

"That's that Doctor Curr's doings, I'll bet," said Nulla.

They quickly tried again to rouse him but Mop just lay there. He definitely isn't going anywhere, thought Darcy.

"We have to go!" said Darcy. "He'll have to wait for another time."

Nulla and Darcy reluctantly left Mop and joined the others.

Billy had a four-wheel drive waiting at the door. Two of the men were just finishing letting the air out of the tyres of all the other vehicles in the car-park.

Lights in the nearby houses came on and people were gathering outside to see what all the fuss was about.

Someone shouted at them.

As the raiders sped from the compound, men could be seen running towards the hospital.

Billy drove straight out into the desert. After some time, they drove past the caves and hid the four-wheel drive in a gully, covering it with sand. Then they back-tracked to the caves.

Deep down in the caves everyone cheered the success of the mission.

"Where's Alma?" asked Nulla.

"She's gone," said Old George. "Left without saying a word."

"How long?"

"About four days - the morning after you were caught."

"I'm going after her," said Nulla. "There's a couple of questions I wouldn't mind asking her."

"You get yourself patched up first," ordered Old George. "There's plenty of time for that later. Anyway, she can't have gone far. She's still green when it comes to the desert."

CHAPTER   EIGHT

Alma had made good time. The desert didn't seem so unfriendly this time round - thanks to Liddy's education.

She occasionally glanced at her own shadow, gliding along the sand beside her. It was the only thing that gave her any sort of company.

Flies never relaxed their assault for one minute. She continually brushed them from her eyes, nose and mouth.

Heat waves shimmered in front of her. The heat distorted the hot sand into pools of water. Yet they always remained well in front, and Alma never could catch up to them.

How long to go? Had it been four days or five, now? She figured it must be two more days at the most, to reach the compound.

Alma had plenty of time to think about what she would say to her parents. A niggling thought in the back of her mind told her that it was useless to try and persuade them. They probably wouldn't listen. Liddy said it had been tried before and they didn't listen then, so why would they listen to a seventeen-year old girl. She couldn't help it if they didn't want to be pulled out of an evil dream, but she felt it was worth the effort. How could she live with herself if she didn't try.

Where would she be now, if she hadn't found that old book? Maybe she would've been better off if she hadn't found it. She'd still be in the tourism workshop.

Alma dawdled along in the mid-day sun.

No! she told herself. How could it be better to stay ignorant? She couldn't go back to that set-up. No better than a robot!

She thought about the city, far off on the coast. What would it be like? The school books had pictures, about places all over the world.

There were even people called Pakistanis and Indians who looked similar to herself. Maybe she could sneak into the city and pretend to be one of them. The authorities wouldn't know the difference.

"What would Sydney be like?" she said aloud.

The old book kept coming to mind - all the different races of people, not really different at all. Except, of course, their colour and features. They were spirits flying around after each death and entering new races of people all the time!

That old book, tucked away under her bed, had really opened her eyes. For the first time in her life, things made sense. It must be the truth! Why else would she be making this effort?

It wouldn't even matter if she were caught. Just to see the city, for one day, would be worth it. All they could do is send her back to the compound. There would be some trouble but that would soon blow over.

A loud buzzing sound distracted her thoughts.

"Oh no!" she said aloud.

Alma looked up to see a small white plane almost directly above her.

She jumped for the nearest cover - a dry spindly bush.

It was too late. The plane circled above her for what seemed like forever.

Alma lay still, but she knew there was trouble ahead.

Finally the plane gave up circling and headed south, probably in the direction of what must've been Broken Hill, the nearest major town. At least she had her bearings confirmed by the plane's departure.

"Stupid girl!" she scolded herself. Old Lloyd, from the compound, had told her to sleep under shelter for two hours in the mid-day heat.

She had been carried away with her day-dreaming. Again!

Alma continued to scold herself as she walked, changing directions every now and then, in the hope of evading a search party.

The rest of the day dragged on forever.

Eventually, a slight cool breeze came with the darkening sky. At first she tossed and turned, worried about being caught, but soon fell off to sleep.

Shortly, she sensed that something was wrong. Was she dreaming again? Someone held her hand. She still had her eyes closed and felt like she was sleeping. But then again, it didn't feel like one of her usual dreams. Someone held her hand and she wanted to pull it away because it didn't feel right.

Alma came out of the deep sleep and briefly saw the bright red insides of her eyelids before opening them.

The sunlight dazzled her for a moment.

A face grinned at her!

A fat ugly face, with small pig-like eyes, looked down at her.

Alma pulled her hand away.

The big black stranger grabbed her by the foot as she tried to escape.

"Leave me alone!" she yelled. Alma kicked and kicked but he held tight, laughing at her weak attempt to get away.

She tried throwing sand in his face but that didn't work. He just closed his eyes and laughed even more.

"Alright," he said. "If you want to do it the hard way." Pulling her back, he grabbed her by the throat with one hand, and punched her in the face.

Everything went white before going completely black. Then the blackness drifted into nothingness.

The next time Alma opened her eyes, he was still there staring at her. No, she thought, it wasn't just a bad dream - it really is happening!

"Now listen very carefully, Morgan." The man pushed up his leather hat slightly. "It's dead or alive for you, and I don't care. So, you just be a good little lady and you might come out the other end in one piece. Alright?"

Alma looked him up and down, trying to figure him out. He must've been roughly the same age as her father, but he was dressed in dirty stained khaki clothes and smelt of stale alcohol. By the look in his eyes, he definitely would carry out his threat.

Because of the sudden shock of capture and the rising fear, Alma decided to do what he wanted.

"Just let go of me and I'll do what you want."

He let go of her leg.

"Right! Start walking in that direction." He pointed to the west.

Alma picked up her bag and began walking. The man followed close behind on his horse. Once, she turned to ask why he was doing this, but all she got was a shove from the horse's nose.

It must've been two hours solid walking before smoke suddenly appeared. A campfire could be seen just up ahead.

A small man stood watching them as they approached the campsite. He held a rifle in one hand.

"She looks better close up, hey Loo?"

"Just tie her up good and tight for now." Loo stepped down from his horse and stretched. "I need a drink."

"Any sign of the others?

"Nope."

"Are we going to take her back or keep on looking?"

Loo took a swig from a bottle of plonk.

"Idiot! Sometimes I just don't know about you, Fish." Loo stared at the little man briefly, then took another swig. He lay down and rested on one elbow. Stretching out near the campfire, he continued:

"Now look, Fish. We got all the time in the world. As long as the grog lasts, we stay out here." He took another swig.

Fish soon realised that he had better get a drink too.

After some heavy drinking and a little food, Fish turned his attention to Alma.

"Want something to eat?"

Alma didn't answer even though she was very hungry.

"Suit yourself," said Fish. "Doesn't say much, hey Loo?"

"I bet she'd sing like a little parrot, after some of this nectar from the gods," laughed Loo. He took another long guzzle.

It was getting dark now. The sun was below the horizon.

Both men were drunk. Fish danced a jig around the campfire. Loo laughed at the little man, which seemed to get him going more.

When he fell into the fire, he decided he'd had enough of the dancing.

Alma didn't like the way they were looking at her.

Loo got up and staggered over. He pulled a knife from his belt, reached down and cut the rope from Alma's hands.

"Get your gear off," said Loo.

Fish rubbed his hands together.

"No way!" Alma sat up, trying to get into a position where she could fight him off.

Fish staggered around behind her.

"Now look little lady. I already told you - either way. Why don't you just relax and enjoy the ride."

Loo took another swig. Fish dived at her legs. Alma kicked, struggling to break his hold. Loo stood and watched.

Fish, even though rotten drunk, still had a good hold. Alma grabbed him by the hair and yanked with all her might. Fish finally let go.

Alma let go of his hair and made a dash for it.

Someone grabbed her by the boot as she half-crawled, half-scrambled for an escape.

It was no use.

She dug her fingers into the sand, trying to stop Loo from dragging her towards the fire.

"Bastards!"

Loo rolled her over by twisting her ankle. Alma lay on her back, screaming at the pain.

The big man jumped onto her chest and pinned her arms under his knees. As he sat on her, he called to Fish:

"Bring that bottle over here."

Loo stuck his finger and thumb into either side of Alma's cheeks and forced her mouth open. When she screamed again, in pain, he poured the plonk down her throat.

"Come on little sister, let's get in the mood." He tightened his grip as she fought to get away from the bottle.

It's useless, thought Alma.

Loo smashed the bottle against her lips and teeth repeatedly. Alma sobbed. There was absolutely nothing she could do.

The foul alcohol flowed down into her. She coughed as she gasped for air.

Fire roared up inside her when the alcohol hit the bottom of her empty stomach. Burning heat spread into every part of her body.

Loo took a swig and handed the bottle to Fish.

"Get her gear off," ordered Loo.

Alma could feel her boots being pulled off. Next, her short pants were pulled down off her legs. Loo ripped her t-shirt down the front.

"Look what we got here!" he laughed.

"Get off me, you bastards!"

Loo punched her in the face and stood up, unbuckling his belt.

"Hold her a minute, Fish."

Alma fought for one last surge of strength. She screamed as she threw handful after handful of sand at Fish.

"Hell!" yelled Fish. His hands went straight for his own face, covering his eyes. But it was too late - he fell to one side, rubbing frantically at his eyes.

"Idiot!" said Loo.

Alma swung around onto her knees and hands. She scrambled away again, in desperation.

Loo brought his boot hard up under her stomach and she groaned uncontrollably as the power of the kick forced all the air from her lungs.

Alma rolled over onto her side, in agony. She couldn't breathe!

Her lungs just would not open. She looked up, trying to anticipate the next blow that she was sure would be on it's way any second now.

It was too late.

A big boot crashed down on her face. Blackness filled her mind. The struggle had ended - she slipped away into darkness.

*

Darkness soon turned to light. What was this? A truck? It followed her as she walked down the dirt track of the compound. It came closer and closer. The roar of the engine filled her ears. There were two people in the truck but she couldn't see them clearly. The sun's reflection on the windscreen hid their faces.

The truck raced up to her. Alma ran to the side. The truck followed. She tripped and fell to the ground. The truck zoomed in on top of her. Now she could see the two men. Loo and Fish! She screamed as the truck ran straight over the top.

Alma sat up, gasping for air. A dizzy head, blocked nose, dry swollen tongue, a terrible pain in her ankle and a fiercely burning sensation in her groin completely engulfed her with misery.

As she looked around, there was no truck anywhere. It had been an awful dream. Loo and Fish! Now she knew where she had seen them before - they used to do the supply run in the compound.

Alma instantly became aware that she was naked.

Where are my clothes? No! Oh no! She wanted to cry but forced herself not to. Quickly glancing all over the campsite she soon spotted her clothes. Loo and Fish slept beside the burnt-out campfire. Empty bottles littered the place.

Millions of stars lit up the night.

No time to feel sorry - must get away! Now!

The rifle! Where the hell is it? She gave up looking for it almost as soon as she began. Panic had set in. Alma grabbed her bag and ran for it.

Even at quite a safe distance, she still flustered while trying to put on her clothes - terrified at the slightest noise. She was sure they had awoken and were right now after her, but as she ran on and on, no-one came.

By early morning Alma had stopped to rest under a tree, completely exhausted. The pain all over her body also prevented her from going on. She took a little food and water.

After a short rest, and the continual thought of Loo, she forced herself to get up and move on.

Which way to go?

Alma decided to go south. Without really working out a plan, it seemed the best choice. Loo would look for her up north - where she had come from - or over in the east towards the compound. She was sure he would.

The footprints left in the sand worried her. She had forgotten to put on the special slippers.

By the time the sun had reached the top of the sky, Alma had made good time. She was well on her way to Broken Hill and hopefully would reach Sydney.

No-one would ever look for her there, she hoped.

Then, with her curiosity about the city satisfied, she could find her way back to the caves.

There was definitely no question of going back to the compound. Loo would have her handed over to the compound prison. And that just couldn't be allowed to happen, thought Alma.

She looked over to the east. There, far off into the distance, she could see a man on a horse. Even at that distance and in spite of the desert heat waves, she knew it could be only one person.

Grief and panic welled up inside.

It wasn't even worth trying to outrun him.

Before the hour was out, Alma was walking in front of the horse once more, getting the occasional nudge from its nose. Loo chuckled at first and then remained silent for the rest of the journey back to the campsite.

CHAPTER   NINE

Campfires lit up the whole of the compound.

Little specks of twinkling light lit up the dark moonless night.

At one of these campfires sat two men - one older than the other.

The older man looked through the smoke at the younger man.

"It's too late. You have come this far," said the black sorcerer, Old Egbert. "Go ahead, eat!"

The young man sat across the other side of the fire. He held his head low.

"I can't do this," he said. "I just can't go through with it."

Old Egbert picked at the sizzling meat on top of the red coals. He stared at the young man while he savoured the sweet juicy meat.

Eventually, he said:

"Eat from the sacrifice or you will not receive the magic power."

The young man squirmed and screwed up his nose. He looked at his cousin's small body, burning on top of the coals of the fire.

The sorcerer, Old Egbert, spoke again:

"It's too late to turn back now. You must taste the flesh. You have killed, now you must finish it - eat!"

He looked at the young man and then continued:

"The black power will give you anything you wish for. It will help you to be chosen as a council man, if that is what you want. All you have to do is eat, and the magic will be yours."

Old Egbert peeled off some flesh. He leaned forward and offered it to the young man.

"Eat!"

The young man took the flesh, closed his eyes and ate.

Old Egbert laughed softly.

The air seemed colder now and the surrounding darkness closed in on them.

"What now?" said the young man.

"You will hear my voice in your mind," whispered the sorcerer. "Whenever I call, you will obey. Now go!"

The young man wiped the fat from his face, jumped up and ran away into the blackness.

Old Egbert laughed loudly, now that the young man had gone. It was the signal for his two assistants to come out of hiding and join him. There was still plenty of the tender meat left over and this luxury didn't happen often in these modern times.

An hour passed.

Old Egbert wiped his scarred and twisted mouth.

He sat cross-legged in front of the dwindling fire and closed his eyes.

The night was very quiet.

Something had been bothering him for some weeks now.

He thought harder, and suddenly an image of a black teenage girl appeared in front of his mind's eye.

He smiled and nodded to himself.

"So! You are The One," he whispered.

His two assistants gazed at the sorcerer's hard old face, aware that an important vision must be taking place.

Old Egbert laughed at their thoughts - he could tell that they held him in awe and that they thought if they made a noise they might disturb him. He knew his minions couldn't upset his line of thought. But! At last! He had found what had been troubling him for quite awhile now.

The vision remained in front of his mind. With eyes still closed, he began singing softly and rocking back and forth. The air had cooled but the ground beneath him held the fire's warmth.

After some time he stopped and opened his eyes.

A black crow, high up in a tree behind them let out an ugly squawk. The two assistants looked around - startled.

Old Egbert held out a skinny arm and pointed his long crooked finger to a spot on the other side of the fire.

The big black crow noisily flapped its wings as it flew down to the spot. Then it pranced around, cocking its head to one side. The shiny black bird peered at the sorcerer for a moment, as if it could read his mind, then looked at the bones lying beside the fire.

Old Egbert began to rock and sing again, staring at the crow. The bird picked at the leftovers.

Shortly it stopped and looked at Old Egbert with one of its fire-red eyes.

With a loud roar the sorcerer yelled:

"Go!"

His arm shot back behind and pointed towards the west.

Old Egbert smiled as the bird flew up and out into the blackness.

The squawking crow disappeared into the dark moonless night.

*

That same night, in another part of the compound, Old Lloyd also sat in front of his campfire. He was alone.

The flames danced around, casting flickering light onto his naked and scarred body.

For two days now he had sung and chanted. Only a short while ago the image came to him. Exhausted from the concentration, he could now relax for he had located the source of the spiritual calling.

Before his mind's eye he could see the girl.

But something was wrong!

A shadow passed over her image. What was it? A crow! He knew that there was evil connected with it.

Intuition guided his mind.

Old Lloyd could finally smile now.

"So! You are The One!" he whispered.

The image unfolded and showed more of what was happening. The old man frowned. The girl is in trouble and needs help, he thought.

Aware that there was no time to spare, he quickly walked to the shack. The image remained before his mind's eye. She was screaming!

In a flash he grabbed the small stick from his leather bag. He reached in again and brought out some strands of human hair. Working quickly he tied the hair to one end of the small stick.

Then he made his way back to the campfire as fast as his old legs could carry him.

When he reached the campfire, Old Lloyd bent down and rubbed his fingers in the hot white ashes of the outer coals. Carefully turning the stick, he painted white stripes around its middle.

Then he concentrated as hard as he could while he attempted to call up an animal-soul from the spirit world.

The light from the fire lit up his face as he conjured up the figure in his mind.

Time was running out!

With a smart step, he pulled his arm back and threw the stick - threw it with all the power that he could muster.

"Go!" he roared.

The stick shot through the air with the strands of human hair trailing behind it.

Before it had gone ten or fifteen feet, the magic stick disappeared into the black night.

Old Lloyd stared after it for a moment. Satisfied that things were as they should be, he resumed his place next to the fire.

He began to sing and chant once more, and his concentration stuck fast on one thing - the desert to the west of the compound.

*

"Take her pants off," Loo chuckled. He sat on Alma's chest, pinning her arms under his knees.

Fish grabbed at her in the dark. The campfire coals faintly glowed in the distance.

Loo took a long swig from a bottle and rammed it into the sand beside Alma. Then he undid his belt buckle.

"Well?" he laughed. "You want it the same way as last night? Or are you going to be a good girl tonight?"

Alma screamed again as she struggled in fear.

Loo forced all his weight down through his knees onto Alma's arms. He put his mouth over hers and Alma nearly vomited from the disgusting smell.

She tried to hold it back again and again but eventually the smell overwhelmed her. Vomit spewed out of her mouth.

It splattered all over Loo's face and down the front of his shirt.

He rolled to the side, wiping his face with his hands.

"Right!" he yelled. "That does it!"

He stood up and raised his big boot. He lined up Alma's head.

She instinctively covered her face with her hands.

A loud noise interrupted him.

"What the hell…?" Loo stopped in his tracks, nearly lost balance and had to bring his foot back down while he looked for the cause of the noise.

A huge black crow suddenly appeared. It noisily flapped its wings and squawked continuously as it flew around the campsite.

Then it darted at Fish, just scraping the top of his head.

Blood poured from the wound.

He dived for the rifle and fired repeatedly into the black night. The crow darted all over the place. Fish tried to follow it with rapid shots.

A bullet narrowly missed Loo.

He dived for cover.

The bird landed beside Alma's head.

She put up her hand for protection.

Fish fired.

Dirt flew into the air only inches from Alma's head.

The bird moved closer to her head.

Fish aimed carefully and squeezed the trigger.

Loo ripped the rifle from his hands as the bullet exploded out of the gun's barrel.

"Idiot!" he yelled. "You nearly killed me!"

"This isn't right!" said Fish. "There's something weird going on here. What's a crow doing out here this time of the night?"

"Shut up idiot!" Loo yelled.

The crow stayed next to Alma's head. Every time she moved away, it hopped closer.

Loo hit Fish in the jaw. His head snapped back as he fell to the dirt.

Loo then grabbed a bottle and took a swig as he eyed-up the crow next to Alma.

He threw the bottle at it. The crow jumped up into the air as the bottle bounced close to Alma's head.

"Damn bird!" he muttered.

Alma made a dash for the desert but Loo was on top of her in an instant.

The squawking crow circled above.

Fish recovered and went for the rifle again.

Loo sat on top of Alma and laughed.

Alma screamed. Her fists pounded against his face.

"Damn woman!"

Loo pulled back his big hand.

"Like I say - I don't care! Either way will do me."

Crack! A loud noise ripped through the air.

Alma jerked in fright. What was that? She expected to be unconscious from Loo's punch.   Where did the noise come from?

She opened her eyes, looked at Loo and then followed his line of sight. He was looking at Fish.

Fish just gave a dumbfounded expression.

Then he searched around the dark perimeter of the campfire - totally bewildered.

"What the hell is this?" scowled Loo. His fist was still cocked above Alma's face.

"I don't like it, Loo," said Fish. "I tell you that there's something funny going on here."

"Shut up!"

Loo - satisfied that there was no longer any danger - looked back down at Alma, underneath him. He started to bring his fist down. Something hit him so violently that he flew off Alma.

Alma saw a flash of white fangs on what appeared to be some kind of animal. It smashed into Loo's ribs, knocked him flat and then disappeared out beyond the ring of darkness that surrounded the campfire.

Total silence followed.

Shortly after, Loo recovered and winced as he rolled onto his back. He yelled across to Fish.

"Shoot it!"

"Where is it? What was it?" Fish panicked, wheeling on the spot with the gun pointed outwards.

Loo half scrambled, half staggered to his feet - partly from the drink and partly from the attack.

"Give it here!" He staggered across to Fish and reefed the rifle out of his grip.

Alma crawled behind one of the saddles lying on the sand. The horses, just behind her, whinnied in fright. She tried to hide from the line of fire.

A terrifying growl came from the darkness.

Then the blur of long white fangs charged out of the darkness again. This time Alma could see ferocious, blood-red eyes. The strange looking animal went straight for Loo again.

Loo swung around to meet it. He was too late!

Thump! Down he went again.

The beast disappeared into the darkness once more. It moved so fast that Alma didn't have a chance of seeing what type of animal it could be.

Fish tried to yank the rifle from Loo's hand. But Loo was already half way to his feet again and pushed him away.

Alma ducked and covered her head with her hands. He fired shot after shot in every direction. When the rifle ran out of bullets, both Loo and Fish stood still in the centre of the campfire.

Silence.

Soon, another growl came from the darkness.

Loo quickly reloaded and fired in that direction.

Another growl from the opposite direction!

He fired over there.

Another loud thud!

Alma glanced over the top of the saddle to see Loo's head whip forward before he crashed to the ground.

The strange beast stood next to the unconscious Loo. It didn't move when Fish back-pedalled out into the darkness of the desert - it just stared at Alma.

She began to tremble.

She had never seen anything so horrible. Eyes full of blood gazed at her.

It wasn't a dingo! Alma had seen pictures of those when she went to the compound school. Anyway, they were now supposed to be extinct.

This beast did resemble something like a dingo though. But, it had white stripes on its body and a striped tail - long, straight and pointed. Strange!

Also, it was too big to be a dingo, though it could've been the same colour.

She thought that it was maybe something like a cross between a dingo and a tiger.

It stood near the fire for a few minutes, panting and staring at Alma.

She froze stiff with fear. Her body began to shake.

What was this thing going to do now?

Eventually, the beast turned and walked out into the desert - the same direction Fish had taken.

Alma lay on the ground for what seemed like hours. Finally she regained her wits, grabbed her clothes and bag, and ran into the dark desert.

With the image of the beast still in her mind, she ran blindly.

A faint squawk came from far off in the distance. Alma gasped, then relaxed a little when she heard an even fainter noise follow the last squawk. The crow had given up too. She ran and ran. Her only thought now was to get far away from that campsite.

With little sleep and no food, she soon slowed to a walk.

The sun took its time climbing up over the horizon.

Patches of small bush trees shone orange as the sunrays bounced off them. Heat blazed down.

Alma hesitated. Was she going north or south? She stopped, looked behind and saw no-one following. Realising she had been on automatic most of the night, she decided to sit down and rest her exhausted body.

North to the caves? Or south to the town of Broken Hill? It didn't matter anymore - as long as it was away from that place and those people.

The desert heat increased.

She knew that the first thing she should do is find water - Liddy had taught her that. Alma wished Liddy were with her now.

"No! I've had enough!" she called out to the lonely desert.   A small bird fluttered off from a nearby tree.

Can't take anymore, she thought. It's useless to try to outrun them. Damn the water. Need sleep. She threw herself down under the nearest tree and closed her eyes. Bright red light filtered through her eyelids.

"Sleep, sleep - go to sleep," she told herself.

The image of the beast wouldn't let her sleep. The fierce red eyes stared at her. It walked over and bit into her hand. It shook her arm violently. White fangs dug deep into her flesh.

Alma willed herself to snap out of the no man's land of dream, between sleep and reality. Sleep! Need sleep! Not dreams!

But wait! Something or someone held her by the hand.

Alma reluctantly opened her eyes.

A black face smiled down on her.

"We meet again," said Nulla.

The smiling white teeth, the big bushy beard, the safety that went with him holding her hand - she felt the tension drain away, and instantly, happiness surged up inside her.

"Nulla!" she whispered.

CHAPTER   TEN

The mouth of the cave was a welcomed sight. It reminded Alma of a huge snake-hole. She walked down the gentle slope into the darkness. A soft cushion of moss felt pleasing under her bare feet.

Laughter and smiles greeted the party of four - Nulla, Darcy, Alma and Billy - as they emerged from the underground river entrance.

Over the next week Alma recuperated from her ordeal. Then she helped Liddy and the other girls gather food out in the nearby desert. Small potato-like yams, berries, roots, lizards and snakes - there was an abundance of food and water when you knew where to look.

She was amazed at how quickly the desert went from a lifeless hell to a land full of richness. As the days flew by, she came to an understanding of 'Mother Earth'. Liddy had told her that 'Mother Earth' was a great spirit that cared for the people. Alma began to sense the presence of this power.

She had told Nulla and Old George about the strange beast, the crow and her two captors.

Old George had just looked straight through her without saying a word.

She wondered if they thought she was going crazy. Maybe she was! Maybe it had been a terrible dream.

Nulla told her about his ordeal in the compound prison.

She thought about her parents still inside that horrible place. What could she do? There was no way she could go back now - not after the nightmare with Loo and Fish.

One morning Alma sat beside her campfire, still brooding over the problem.

Nulla walked over and joined her.

"A couple of us are going for a walk," he said. "Want to come?"

Alma snapped out of her misery. Nulla was always laughing and it made her feel good.

A dog wandered over close to them. Nulla whistled and gave him a pat.

"I think the word has got around. Looks like we'll have an extra along." He smiled and pointed to the dog.

The dog wagged his tail and nuzzled into Nulla's hand.

"What do you think, Alma? Should we let young Turk here come with us?"

She laughed as the dog began to whine.

"I don't think you have a choice."

"Yeah."

Nulla patted the dog some more.

Alma looked at young Turk. His eyes were smiling. It reminded her of something, but she couldn't quite put her finger on it. Then it hit her.

The beast in the desert! That was it. Young Turk reminded her of the striped beast out in the desert.

Those eyes! It was as if she had recognised something in the beast's eyes, but fear at the time had prevented her from understanding it.

Why didn't it attack her?

Alma looked at Nulla.

"Where are you going?"

"A special place."

Nulla stood up and waved a hand.

"Come on!"

Alma followed behind as he walked to the far end of the cave. There, at another campfire sat Liddy and Freddie.

Nulla picked up a spear and a small bag.

"You ready?"

"Let's go." said Freddie. He jumped up, grabbed a bundle of sticks that had been tied together, and joined Nulla.

All four headed off into the next cave. Nulla led the way, carrying a flaming torch, with the dog trotting along beside him.

Light from the torch flickered and lit up the walls and high rock ceiling.

This place must be millions of years old, thought Alma. She couldn't hear if the river flowed or not - it was dark, but she could sense that it silently moved along beside them.

Something brushed past her hair. The sound of flapping wings startled her.

Liddy laughed when she saw Alma jerk her head to the side.

"Bats."

Alma looked up.

Above her, little black shadows darted here and there.

Voices and other noises echoed high up and far off into the distance.

They walked for what seemed like hours - travelling from one gigantic cave to another, then into another and another.

Just as she started to get used to the dark and wet underworld, a light appeared up ahead.

Gradually the darkness disappeared behind them. Alma followed the others through a small tunnel and stopped in her tracks, staring at the most beautiful sight she had ever seen.

Flowers!

Greens, reds, yellows and gold, pinks and purples - all the brightest and richest colours in the world, surrounding the crystal clear water of a pond. The colourful flowers covered the cave floor and magnificent trees reached up towards the sunlight that shone down through a gaping hole in the roof of the cave.

She thought of the burnt red sand of the desert up above, the withered and stunted trees, and the intense heat of the sun.

Mouth wide open, she stood staring at the wonderland.

Rays of sunlight shot down onto the still water and bounced back up to the roof of the cave to give the effect of a glittering dome.

The river expanded into a wide pool and then continued on through to the next dark cave.

Small birds, bees and insects hovered and darted about the place. A splash in the water broke the spell. Alma moved towards the pool to investigate.

There it was again!

A fish jumped up out of the water and slowly drifted in mid air before crashing back down into the water. Ripples of water circled out to the edges of the pool.

Nulla, Freddie and Liddy had already taken off what little clothing they were wearing and made their way into the water.

Nulla and Freddie sprayed and splashed each other. Liddy laughed and squealed.

"Come on!" shouted Nulla.

Alma hesitated. No-one but her parents had seen her naked. She felt uneasy. Then the thought of the ordeal in the desert - with Loo and Fish - crept into her mind. They had seen her naked. But most of the ordeal was a complete blank!

They were so cruel. They had no feelings whatsoever about other people's rights. Animals! Even though she couldn't remember a thing about it, she felt unclean.

It wasn't very hard to guess what had happened.

Suddenly, anger rose up inside her. Bastards! You're not going to ruin the rest of my life. I won't let you!

A strange surge of excitement rushed up through her body. The urge to join the others pushed her into action. Before she had any more time to think herself into another state of despair, her clothes were off and she was jumping.

It was magic!

Streams of sunlight warmed the top half of the water while her feet paddled in the colder depths.

Nulla swam over towards her. He gave her a cheeky smile.

A spray of water hit her in the face. She closed her eyes briefly and felt two hands push down on the top of her head.

Under she went!

Alma struggled, without success. Then, in desperation, she ducked under and away from his hands, to swim to safety.

Nulla chased her across the pool.

She dived at him, splashing frantically. He disappeared under the surface.

Alma circled and searched for him in the clear water.

She screamed as his hands clasped tight around her ankles. He up-ended her and the screams died in a mouth full of water.

The other two joined in. A water fight between the two couples ended in an explosion of spray. The girls squealed and the young men shouted at each other.

Then Liddy jumped up onto Freddie's shoulders. Alma squealed louder when Nulla slipped under the water and slid in between her legs. Shortly, she rose up out of the water too, to face Liddy.

Freddie drove hard through the water towards Nulla. Liddy clenched Alma's hands. They laughed as they struggled, trying to topple each other.

Liddy got the upper hand and Alma crashed into the water with a splash.

"One down!" laughed Freddie. "Best of five."

This time, as Freddie drove forward, Nulla side-stepped. Alma nearly lost her balance but just managed to hold on, grabbing at Nulla's hair.

Liddy and Freddie disappeared under the water.

"You tripped me!" shouted Freddie when he resurfaced.

Nulla laughed. "One each."

Half an hour later, Liddy declared her team the winners.

Exhausted, everyone paddled off in different directions and rested as they soaked up the glorious sunshine.

Never, in all her life, had Alma enjoyed herself so much before.

She ran her hands through the warm clear water. It was paradise.

Gradually the light faded as the sun disappeared from above. Shadows reached out across the pool.

Nulla was the first out. He built a fire with the bundle of dry sticks.

One by one, the others joined him. The warmth from the flames mixed with the cold air of the caves.

After a quick lunch, Liddy and Freddie didn't waste any time - they cuddled and soon were passionately kissing. Alma felt slightly uneasy at their open display of affection. She turned away and watched the bees buzzing from flower to flower, the birds darting from insect to insect and the tiny ripples race across the surface of the pool as the dog snatched at the jumping fish.

Nulla picked up some stones and threw them to the dog. Young Turk looked so funny with his head the only visible part above the surface of the water. He would vigorously chew every stone that he caught until another came sailing through the air. Then he would roll it out the side of his mouth with his tongue just in time to catch the next one.

Nulla looked at Alma and they laughed at the antics of the dog.

He stopped and took her hand.

They gazed into each other's eyes.

The campfire gave off a loud bang as a spark exploded and shot out into the darkness.

The stillness and the silence of the massive cave crept in, once more, to take control as the night approached.

It was time to leave.

Alma's troubles and emotions had left her for that brief magical moment. She felt at peace as she followed the others back through the dark caves.

A short distance from the main camp, Alma could hear music and singing.

Is it a celebration? The night was well on its way. She wondered what it could be for.

As the two couples walked closer, men coated in white ash could be seen dancing around a flaming campfire. Women sat in a circle surrounding the prancing men. The old women rocked from side to side and tapped sticks together as they chanted to the rhythm of the dance. Younger men, girls and children looked on as the dancers shook spears high in the air and acted out what appeared to be mock battles.

Alma had never seen anything like this at the compound. She was sure that the people from Australwitz One would come to their senses and join the rebels if they witnessed this freedom. The dance stirred emotions inside her that she couldn't understand - but it left her in exhilaration.

Why do the people in the compound just sit there and take what's dished out to them?

She had even tried to get her father to read the old book, but he just smiled and shook his head.

"Not for me, love," he had said. "I'm happy enough as it is. I don't need any of the white man's wisdom."

Tiredness set in as the dance came to a close.

Alma drifted off to sleep next to her campfire.

Nulla greeted her in the morning. Liddy and the other girls had already left.

He touched her hand. They sat in silence for some time.

Eventually, Alma asked:

"What was the celebration for?"

"It was a celebration of the moon - The Moon Dance. Old George can explain it much better - ask him the next time you see him."

He remained silent for awhile and then spoke again:

"It was good, yesterday. What do you think?"

Alma didn't speak. A powerful magnetic force pulled her towards Nulla - she wanted to cling to him. Once again, strange emotions surged up through her body. She could feel her soul reaching out over to his.

Something like electricity shot up through his hand and into her body. Alma tingled all over.

She gritted her teeth.

"I can't."

Nulla looked at her for a moment, slowly nodded and then took his hand away from hers.

"Fair enough. I just thought after yesterday we could be... Is there a reason?"

"I don't know why? It's just that... I can't explain it. I'm sorry."

Tears filled her eyes and she began to shake. She tried to control her emotions so that Nulla wouldn't see the state she was in, but he had already stood up and was walking away. Alma felt relief at being left to her own emotions but at the same time grief overwhelmed her when she realised what she had just done. He would never speak to her again.

She sat there for a long time, no thoughts, just complete blankness.

Old George, the tribal elder, interrupted her.

"What did you think of the dance last night?" he said with a smile.

"It was magical - it made me feel alive."

Old George smiled a knowing smile.

"Do you like it here with us?"

"I love it."

"Why do you want to leave then?"

"How did you know?"

"I've seen it many times. It's written all over your face."

Alma blushed and looked away.

She forced herself to look at the old man when he just continued to sit there in silence.

The snowy white beard and the white hair were a rare sight on a black man these days but it gave him a sort of powerful presence. Alma liked being near him.

"Many have had their own reasons for wanting to leave. What's yours?"

"I want to go to the city - just to see what it's like. Then I'll come back."

Old George smiled and thought for awhile before talking again.

"Some have done that and never returned. A few did make it back. Most got caught and ended up in the prison at the compound. Not a pretty sight once you've been in there."

Alma told him about the book and how it had changed her life.

"I'm not going to try and change your mind, but there is an old story that goes way back to the days when life was simple. Maybe it can help you work things out so that you feel at peace about your decision to make this journey. Do you want to hear it?"

Alma nodded, then said:

"Did you ever go to the city?"

"Yes, I went for a trip with your grandfather, once - that was before the electric fences went up around the compound. We took a holiday from shearing and spent a few days in Sydney."

He laughed as he recalled the trip. Then he continued:

"Don't tell the young ones around here though. You know how they get silly ideas in their heads."

Alma laughed.

He went on:

"I am very old now, but when I was young we heard many stories about our ancestors. Most of the older legends have been forgotten.

"The young ones don't care about these things. They think the old people's stories are just fairytales and they can't see the point."

He stroked his long white beard, looked up at the roof of the cave and continued:

"There is a story that tells about some of our past. My grandfather told me a long time ago. Would you like to hear that one?"

Alma smiled and nodded.

Old George continued:

"Don't get me wrong - I won't try to change your mind. But maybe it will help in your travels."

Old George stoked up the campfire, then began the story.

"This is the story of the old people -

"Long ago, the spirit-beings - our ancestors - took on animal forms.

"For a long time they lived in harmony.

"Then came evil.

"Mother Earth became angry and turned, tilting to one side.

"North and South changed and oceans threw up their waters to wash away the evil of the lands.

"Only a few of the animal-beings survived.

"They lived on the highest mountains where the waters could not reach them.

"After a very long time, the waters slid back to leave new lands and the spirit-beings took on animal forms once more.

"Time had travelled a full circle and was now ready to begin a new cycle.

"This was not so long ago.

"This new time was called The Time of the Death Adder - the time of the poisonous snake.

"The spirit-beings took the form of the dove and they lived in harmony for a very long time. They were of one colour but as the lands divided more and more, the birds also divided into different colours.

"Then one day, seven black vultures appeared in the sky.

"They came from outer space - from a hot, red planet far away.

"Soon their cousins - the black crows - followed and joined the vultures in the sky.

"These evil birds invaded the northern lands of Mother Earth.

"Some of the luckier white doves of the north escaped and flew to the safety of the other lands - to live with their brothers and sisters in the south, east and west.

"It wasn't long before the vultures destroyed the northern lands with their evil ways.

"They needed new lands.

"So, they plotted to invade the other lands.

"By this time the spirit-beings of the other lands had begun to take on new animal forms.

"The cunning vultures first sent their cousins - the black crows - to the southern land to find out how strong these new animals had become.

"Ten black crows flew south.

"When they arrived, one of the crows put on a mask and pretended to be a mighty bird of prey - a falcon.

"The black beings, and their new white brothers that had fled from the north, now living in the south, were easily tricked by this mask - they believed that the falcon was their friend.

"He became their leader.

"By then many black crows had invaded and it was now too late to stop them.

"That was not so long ago.

"Four generations ago, a great white eagle - with big piercing eyes and bushy black eyebrows - had been watching from a cold planet not too far away.

"He decided to fly down to Mother Earth and try to help the black and white beings of the southern land get rid of the crows.

"All the beings of the southern land saw that the white eagle was more powerful than the falcon.

"So they took him for their new leader.

"The crows flew back to the northern lands empty-handed. This made the vultures angry now that they could not steal from the southern land.

"Before long, the cunning vultures sent another crow. He wore the mask of a great white eagle.

"The black and white beings couldn't tell the difference between the two eagles.

"Trouble soon started up.

"The crow tricked the black and white beings into believing that the eagle from the cold planet was no good.

"Sadly, the good eagle was cast out.

"He felt sorry for the black and white beings, but what could he do?

"By the time the black and white beings found out that the crow tricked them, it was too late - swarms of black crows had returned to steal from them and ruin the southern land.

"Some of the black and white beings tried to trick the crows.

"They wore masks that made them look like parrots and sparrows and even a chicken hawk!

"But the crows were too cunning to fall for that old trick.

"Harmony turned to bitterness and sadness in the southern land.

"That is why they called it the time of The Death Adder - the time of the poisonous snake.

"The black and white beings longed for the great white eagle to return from the cold planet but he would not.

"He knew that he alone couldn't fight the cunning vultures and their cousins, the crows.

"At the same time, the vultures, through their black crow cousins, had also taken over the eastern lands.

"Now, their cousins - the crows - stole from most of the lands of Mother Earth.

"They took everything back to their masters - the vultures - in the northern lands.

"The great white eagle had come down about four generations ago.

"But just before that, over in the eastern lands - about five generations ago - another great being had also been watching Mother Earth.

"He had been watching the eastern land.

"This great being - in the shape of a giant red lion - flew down from the sun. He came to help the beings of the eastern land.

"He stood on the highest mountain of the land and let out a mighty roar.

"It was so powerful that it shook the earth.

"The black crows were so frightened, they flew back to the vultures in the northern land.

"The cunning vultures laughed and sent a crow wearing a mask of a lion.

"Of course, the beings became confused at the sight of two giant red lions.

"But the lion from the sun was too smart for the crow. With one swipe of his huge powerful paw, he tore the mask from the crow.

"The giant red lion then taught the beings of the eastern land how to protect themselves from the vultures and crows.

"When he knew that they could look after themselves, he flew back up to the sun and now watches over them.

"The vultures still rule the northern, southern and western lands but dare not go near the eastern land.

"I have seen it written in the sky that the giant red lion from the sun will send someone to help us in our southern land.

"It is also written that the vultures and crows will pay heavily for their evil ways.

"This will happen soon!

"And the beings on Mother Earth will live in harmony once more!

"This is the story of the old people."

Old George looked at Alma and smiled.

PART TWO

CHAPTER ONE

Doctor Curr stood in front of the full-length mirror, in his office. He looked at his reflection - white coat, grey trousers, black shoes, glasses, balding head and all of his four-foot-eleven inches of height.

He turned side-on and took another look. His new shoes, with thicker soles and heels, didn't make the slightest difference to his height.

Slowly he tried to square up his rounded shoulders and push out his flat chest. It didn't make any difference.

I must be getting old, he thought. But there are still signs of the Aryan-German stock, despite the old age. A trace of a smile appeared on his face.

Today is going to be a good day, he thought. I've been waiting along time for this - the Sydney Conference!

Doctor Curr ambled over to his desk and sat down in the big leather chair. He threw one leg up onto the top of the desk, and rolled up his trouser-leg.

Then he reached into the top drawer and grabbed the hypodermic needle. Within seconds he filled it and gave himself the daily injection.

He waited for the bing!

It didn't come - as usual.

Thirty years had gone by, after that first big buzz, and it had never occurred again.

The deadness slowly spread throughout his body. His hands stopped shaking. And when he couldn't feel his tongue on the roof of his mouth he knew it had taken hold.

"The big day!" The psychiatrist eased himself out of the chair and headed for the daily rounds of the compound complex.

Nurse Shelley met him in the corridor.

He took the clip-board from her hand and quickly scanned the pages.

"Mop Thomson can go back to the compound," he said. "Rehabilitation is complete."

Nurse Shelley nodded and then followed the doctor on the hospital rounds.

He didn't waste any time today - for he had to get away early, to catch the plane to Sydney.

Within minutes Doctor Curr and Nurse Shelley were back at reception.

"Well! I'll see you when I get back from the conference. You have my number if there are any problems."

The doctor was already heading for the Supply Depot before he had finished the sentence.

"Excuse me, Doctor!" Nurse Shelley called down the corridor after him. "There's one more thing."

"Yes." He turned impatiently.

She pointed towards the last hospital bed.

"You missed this patient. I'm sorry. I should've mentioned it earlier.

"Jimmy doesn't seem to be responding to the increased dosage."

Doctor Curr snatched at the clipboard and shuffled through the pages.

Jimmy sat up in bed as they approached. He mumbled something and stared off into space.

"Hmm." Doctor Curr rubbed his chin while he read the patient's details on the clipboard.

He looked at the black man sitting in the hospital bed.

"Increase the dose to double strength and make a note of any side-effects. We'll add this patient to the new trial that I recently started."

He handed the clipboard to Nurse Shelley.

As he turned to leave, Jimmy called after him.

"Devils and Snakes! They won't leave me alone."

The doctor looked at Nurse Shelley and then at Jimmy. With curly black hair covering his eyes, the patient quickly glanced from side to side. He brushed at the white bed-sheet and continued to mumble to himself.

Doctor Curr had seen it all before. It was a classic case. He turned away and walked toward the Supply Depot.

After pouring the sterilizing-liquid into the drinking water outlet that fed the compound, he quickly locked the cabinet and re-traced his steps through the hospital toward the prison wing.

Tom Martin - the prison manager - stood at the door of his office as Doctor Curr approached.

"Now listen carefully, Tom," said the doctor.

The prison manager lifted his nose and looked down at him.

Doctor Curr introverted for a brief moment before snapping out of it and reclaiming his authority. He knew all about Tom's little game of dominating people with his size. But even more importantly he also knew who was the overall compound manager.

Doctor Curr took a step forward, looked up and continued:

"You are the manager of this prison. I don't want to hear any excuses. Yes - the nurse did let the rebels in, and yes - the rebels did catch your night-guards on the wrong foot. But, you're in charge of the whole operation - you should've known or at least expected something like this to happen. I can't be watching over your shoulder all the time. I have my own duties to attend to. Now, I'm going away for a few days and I want you to double the guards on nightshift. Also, no one is allowed to touch the new security system while I'm away - keep the line to the Broken Hill police station open. There better not be any trouble or it'll be your head that's on the chopping block - not mine."

"Yes sir," said Tom Martin. He had come down an inch or two.

Doctor Curr turned and walked back down the corridor, briefly glancing at the prisoners in their cells.

A soft flutter of noise behind him caught his attention. He glanced to his side and saw Tom's reflection in an office window.

The prison manager had been following him on tip-toes and holding his fingers up behind the doctor's head.

Doctor Curr halted abruptly and swung around.

The prison manager quickly extended his hand and reached for the door.

"Have a nice trip, sir," he smiled.

The doctor stared at him briefly before shaking his head at the idiocy of the man, then left the prison.

It wasn't a long trip into Broken Hill. Glad to see the back end of this barren land for a few days, he thought.

He sighed with relief as the plane shuddered along the runway and then lifted into the air.

The big day!

Finally!

All these years and finally the International Psychiatric Convention was going to be held in Australia.

The Australian Psychiatric Association will most undoubtedly put on a spectacular show for our northern colleagues, he mused.

Doctor Curr eased himself back into the first class seat. Time to relax!

One of the many newspapers, lying at his side, caught his eye.

He picked it up and read:

'230 BILLION DOLLAR DEFICIT

TAXES WILL GO UP AGAIN'

He then dismissed the rest of the article and flicked through the paper. Nothing of note caught his attention other than the full frontal nudes of males and females on every second page.

Putting it to the side, he grabbed another newspaper and read:

'USSF of GERMANY BUYS INTO AUSTRALIA'

'The United States of the Supreme Fatherland of Germany now owns most of Australian Mining. Record profits are said to be as high as 250 billion dollars since the German take-over.'

Doctor Curr couldn't be bothered with the rest of the article and quickly flicked through the remaining pages. Full frontal nudes of males and females covered every second page but other than that nothing worthwhile leaped out at him.

He grabbed another paper. It started with headlines of:

'GERMAN BANK LOANS for AUSTRALIAN GOVT.

The USSF of Germany rescues Australian recession.'

And the rest of the paper had been adorned with the usual full frontal nudes of male and female bodies - the odd body catching the doctor's eye.

Another newspaper with headlines of:

'PERVERTS TARGET 14 YR OLD BOYS'

"Hmm, this could be interesting," said Doctor Curr. He flattened out the paper to make it easier to read. The plane lurched and his stomach jumped into his mouth.

When the plane had passed the slight turbulence he read on:

'Despite disapproval from the Lords and the majority of the English population, the Government goes ahead and revises the law on homosexuality. From today, the legal age of consent for homosexual encounters will be 14 years of age.'

Doctor Curr threw the newspaper down in disgust.

He mumbled to himself.

"Homosexuality is not a perversion!

"Psychiatry proved that gays were normal!"

He shook his head.

"Where is this propaganda coming from?"

He snatched at the paper. Ah! American newspaper! The United States of Spiritual Freedom for America sticking its nose in where it's not wanted - once again.

"Damn the USSF of America!" As he threw the paper down an Air Steward pulled up next to him in the isle.

"Any refreshments, sir?" lisped the steward. He wore heavy eye shadow, earrings, lip-stick and painted fingernails.

The blonde steward leant forward and laid his hand on the doctor's arm. A whiff of strong perfume filled the immediate area.

"No thank you," said the doctor. He forced a smile and pulled his arm away.

"Ooh! Are you sure now?" said the steward, showing a rather wide gap in his front teeth as he smiled.

When the doctor didn't answer, the steward bent his wrist and then continued to push the trolley down the isle.

"Refreshments, madam?" lisped the steward as he continued on his way.

The perfume clung to the insides of the doctor's nostrils. He felt as if he had been molested by a smell.

The plane started its descent.

Thirty minutes later the chauffeur drove out of the airport and shortly after that unloaded Doctor Curr in front of the APA headquarters - the Australian Psychiatric Association headquarters.

A noisy group of people, carrying posters, marched in a circle and chanted in front of the skyscraper.

"Down with psychiatry!"

"Psychiatry kills!"

"Psychiatry is a fraud!"

One of the protesters caught the doctor's attention. When he recognised who the protester was, he quickly scuttled in through the massive entrance. He hoped that Fred - the ex-trainee of psychiatry - didn't recognise him.

The president of the APA, Doctor Hapsburg, greeted Doctor Curr with a handshake as he entered the top floor office.

The third person in the room, another psychiatrist, remained in his seat but this didn't bother Doctor Curr. After all! That other psychiatrist just happened to be the Head of all psychiatric associations across the planet and none other than the infamous Doctor Hanover himself.

Doctor Hapsburg, who stood above Doctor Curr by about three inches, retreated to the bar and poured three brandies.

Doctor Curr felt a little drab in his grey suit - that is, compared to the expensive black pinstripe suit of Doctor Hapsburg, and the even more expensive white suit of Doctor Hanover.

As the drinks were handed out, Doctor Hapsburg said:

"Good afternoon, Herr Curr. You've met Herr Hanover, of course."

They nodded and smiled at each other. Then Curr and Hapsburg sat down to enjoy their drinks.

"This is the man handling the Aboriginal Final solution, isn't it?" said Hanover.

"Yes," said Doctor Hapsburg. "Herr Curr runs Australwitz One and Herr Grolsh runs Australwitz Two. You'll meet Grolsh at the convention."

"And how is the glorious Fatherland, Herr Hanover?" said Doctor Curr.

Hanover licked at the brandy that had found its way onto his short black moustache and smiled:

"The Fatherland is as glorious as ever! And Berlin will always be the central point of the entire universe!"

All three laughed and drank in agreement. Hapsburg rose to replenish the empty glasses.

Hanover continued:

"The USSF of Germany has recently extended its borders to Siberia in the east and Spain in the west. We, of course, already have England, but Scotland and Ireland are continuing to be their usual thick-headed selves. Must be that flawed red-haired gene still causing problems for the race."

Curr and Hapsburg grunted in approval as the drinks were handed out.

Hanover gulped at the brandy, licked his moustache and went on:

"I hope everything is in order for the convention tonight? The new electric shock machine is ready? Has the other film been made yet?"

Hapsburg smiled:

"Yes sir. Herr Curr will be overseeing the making of the backup film this afternoon. The new Super Seven Electro Shocker is already at my private hospital and we have a suitable patient for the film. The convention will thoroughly enjoy the little surprise we have in store for them tonight."

Hanover busied himself mopping up a brandy stain on his white trousers. When he was satisfied, he said:

"What time will the convention finish tonight?"

"About midnight. Why do you ask, sir? Do you have to be somewhere, later tonight?" said Hapsburg.

"No. No. It's just that my health has been failing me recently." Hanover gulped the rest of the brandy and handed the empty glass to Hapsburg. "Yes. It's all this unrest in the Fatherland."

"Yes! We've been kept informed, although not fully." Hapsburg returned with full glasses of brandy. "Most of it has been censored by the time it reaches our southern continent. Even so, I do know of the American Resistance and their latest spy network. No sooner do we expand our territory across Europe and right on our trail come the Yankee revolutionaries."

The brandy helped Curr pluck up enough courage to join the conversation.

"Can't the German Secret Service do anything?"

"There is talk that the Americans have a new listening satellite system - our experts believe it is some sort of laser infiltration," whispered Herr Hanover.

He looked up at the ceiling and continued.

"They think it can even penetrate walls and eavesdrop on any conversation."

Doctor Curr looked up at the ceiling and imagined a beam coming down from some remote satellite out in space. He shook his head at the possibility of such a thing.

"Amazing!" said Hapsburg. He was standing, reaching out for empty glasses.

The phone rang. Hapsburg signalled for Doctor Curr to take over at the brandy cabinet while he answered the call.

"Yes? … How long has this been going on? … Well why wasn't I told earlier? …Get the Police Investigation Groundforce. Urgently!"

Hapsburg hung up. Herr Hanover asked:

"Problem?"

"No. Just a small matter to clear up." Then he mumbled: "Damn swine protesters."

Doctor Curr handed out the brandy and Hapsburg turned on the security view-screen.

A picture of the protesters, below in the street, flashed onto the wide screen.

"Nazi Psychiatrists Go Home!" The chants blasted out of the view-screen speakers. Hapsburg adjusted the volume.

Doctor Curr noticed that the crowd had increased. Not exactly what we want on the day of the big convention, he thought.

Hapsburg had the phone in hand again.

"Get your team over here immediately! ... I don't care! ... If this matter isn't cleared up within ten minutes, I'll be speaking to the Justice Minister and you - my friend - will be flat-footing it around the streets in the very near future. Of course, that's if you're lucky!"

Doctor Curr quickly scribbled something on the desk notepad and Hapsburg read it while listening on the phone. He then spoke into the mouthpiece again.

"It has just been brought to my attention that the leader of the protesters is a man by the name of Fred Winton. Lock up all the protesters except for the ringleader. Send him to my private hospital, with a guard. Is that clear, Superintendent?"

Hapsburg hung up the phone and looked at Doctor Curr.

"Do you know this fellow called Winton, Herr Curr?"

"I know of him, sir."

"You will make sure that we don't have any more trouble from him, won't you, Herr Curr   ?"

"He will get a thorough psychiatric evaluation, sir."

All three chuckled, raised their glasses and drank their brandy.

Hanover was mopping at another stain on his white suit. When he had finished, he crossed his legs and spoke:

"Now, gentlemen. Let's get down to the real task of this meeting. That protest, which we just now witnessed, is the tip of the iceberg.

"Our real concern is this new political movement that is currently threatening our Australian operation."

Hapsburg handed out more brandy.

"Go on, Herr Hanover," he said.

"If my information is correct, you have a new political party in the making. The Ned Kelly Party or something like that. And what is the name of their leader?"

He looked at Hapsburg.

"Geoff Whitman, sir."

"Yes! That's the fellow. My sources tell me that this political party is relatively minor but is gaining support day by day. It needs to be knocked on the head before the situation gets out of hand. I don't need to remind you gentlemen of the fact that we don't need anti-German and anti-Psychiatry propaganda stirring up trouble at this crucial stage of our operations."

"Yes, of course, sir," said Hapsburg. "What do you suggest?"

"We are so close to having complete control of this sector. The Australian Coalition is now full of our people. We have the government in the palms of our hands. Tonight's convention will win over the remaining ministers. I want this Geoff Whitman committed to your private hospital as soon as possible. There will be information leaked to the press about this fellow and the Justice Department will order that he be detained and given a complete psychiatric evaluation. Your job is to see that he is silenced forever - never to utter a single intelligible word to anyone for the rest of his sorry existence. Do I make myself clear, gentlemen?"

"Yes sir," said Hapsburg. Doctor Curr nodded in agreement.

Herr Hanover, the International President of Psychiatry, stood up and brushed at the front of his stained white suit.

"Good! Very good." He smiled and headed for the door. "See you at the convention tonight."

When he had left, both men sat down again.

Doctor Curr could feel the effects of the brandy taking hold. He had a lot of work to do before the convention and thought it wise to leave now, while he was able to.

The phone rang.

"Yes? ... What! ... How could the damn thing go missing? ... Someone will pay for this! ... I don't care! Get the display model from the convention hall over to the hospital. Urgently! Doctor Curr is on his way."

Hapsburg hung up and shook his head.

"What is it?" asked Doctor Curr.

"The Super Seven Shocker! Someone stole it from the hospital. Can you believe that?"

"Impossible. You can't get the staff these days. I'm on my way over shortly. I'll wager that someone has moved it to another part of the hospital."

"I've sent for the display model from the hall."

"Good. I'll be off then."

The phone rang again.

Hapsburg looked up at the ceiling and shook his head in disbelief. Doctor Curr halted on his way out, but Hapsburg shushed him out the door.

It didn't look good, thought Doctor Curr. This recent news was a bad omen. The elevator dropped to the ground floor and he stepped out into the lobby. He wiped at his brow with a handkerchief. The brandy was well in to the system now.

The Police Investigation Groundforce vans were loading the last of the protesters as he left the building. A large crowd of onlookers hissed and booed at the police.

Someone threw a bottle and sprayed Doctor Curr with beer. He wiped at his grey suit but then quickly realised his time would be better spent dashing to the waiting limousine.

Doctor Curr stared out through the tinted window at the angry mob.

As the big black car drove off, he pictured Fred Winton locked in one of the hospital's cells. Well Mister Winton, he thought, we won't be getting any more trouble from you very shortly. Will we now?

Doctor Hapsburg's private hospital stood in all its majestic glory among a forest of well-watered eucalyptus trees. Colourful flowers and rose bushes surrounded the brilliant white building.

A magnificent weeping willow tree took centre stage out in front of the hospital complex.

The limousine dropped Doctor Curr at the entrance. He marvelled at the most expensive building in all of Australia.

*

Lights flashed.

Buzzers buzzed.

Switches clicked on and off. Metal instruments clanged against metal trays. Nursing staff rushed to and fro.

Home sweet home!

Doctor Curr smiled as he walked into the Electro Convulsive Therapy Unit.

The brandy had reached numbing proportions. His feet paddled their way to the controls. The little psychiatrist was glad to find a seat - his body felt heavy and his head pulsed.

He nodded in approval at the sight of the replacement electric shock machine. Yes! The Super Seven Shocker! The latest development, state of the art piece of equipment - just recently re-introduced back into mental hospitals after years and years of controversy, and battles, with Human Right's Groups. Finally, they had one the hardest battle. Now, with huge Government grants and masses of public money, the psychiatric profession could go ahead and rehabilitate the whole of civilisation.

Not only that, but the salaries would skyrocket. The timing was perfect, thought Doctor Curr. Three years till retirement! Then it's off to the beloved Fatherland to sit out the remainder of life on the golf course.

The Super Seven Shocker sat on a stainless steel trolley next to the ECT-Operating table. The machine sparkled.

A portable hospital bed could be heard approaching, out in the corridor.

It entered the ECT Unit.

"Excuse me, Doctor Curr," said the film cameraman. He wore a peculiar black and white striped baseball cap. "Bad news."

"Don't tell me. There's something wrong with your equipment?"

"No. It's the Berlin film. It's been stolen, along with the other Super Seven."

"You're not serious?"

"I rang Doctor Hapsburg at headquarters and he said to use today's backup film for the convention, tonight."

"I honestly don't believe it."

"I had the English dub-in completed, on the Berlin film, and it was all set for tonight but then one of the nurses discovered that the cabinet had been broken into and it had been taken. We'll just have to use today's backup film as the main attraction, instead of an addition like it was originally intended."

Doctor Curr shook his head at the floor and waved the film man away.

Two huge male psychiatric nurses had wheeled the trolley up to the operating bed.

A girl, of about fourteen, was lifted from the portable bed onto the operating table. Her hospital robe was removed. She lay drugged and naked on the table.

Wide straps were thrown across the body of the young patient. Her long blonde hair flowed over the sides of the table. One of the male nurses pulled at a strap with all his weight.

Doctor Curr waddled over and lifted one of her eyelids with his thumb.

He peered at her dilated pupil, and satisfied, let go of the eyelid. Then he slapped her across the face, waiting for a reaction. When it was obvious that the patient was out cold he turned and said:

"Good! Patient is ready. Let's begin."

Two assistants moved in closer to the bed.

Doctor Curr moved to the side and sat his weary body on a stool. This is ridiculous, he thought. What am I doing here? These hospital staff should be able to do this without my help. Waste of my time. He anxiously drummed the side bench with his fingers.

Various cameras located around the room were switched on. Red lights flashed. The film man gave a thumb's-up.

A psychiatric nurse opened the young girl's mouth, pulled out her tongue, and after piercing a hole, threaded some string through it and pinned it to the outside of the cheek.

Next he manoeuvred a rubber mouth guard over the teeth and closed the young girl's lips as best he could.

Meanwhile the other nurse was just finishing securing all the straps across head, neck, shoulders, chest, waist and legs.

An oxygen tube was pushed down one of the nostrils and monitoring leads were taped to her body.

The Doctor's drumming fingers could now be heard by all - he was impatient, film or no film, and didn't care who knew.

This is taking too long!

"Come on!" he shouted.

The nurses became more active and quickly attached the electrodes to the girl's head.

When everything was in order, both nurses nodded at the doctor, then slowly backed away from the table. They stared at the patient.

The doctor looked at his watch and rubbed his forehead. This is taking too long! He waddled over to the operating table, snatched the hypodermic needle from the female nurse and thrust it into the patient's neck.

As he made his way back to the control panel, the needle rolled off the side bench and smashed onto the floor.

He looked around the room.

Cameras were filming. The staff stood in their proper positions. The patient was ready. And the SS shock machine awaited his command.

Doctor Curr pushed the little red button.

The body of the young girl jerked rigid and then shook violently - twisting uncontrollably, despite the heavy straps.

Her head arched up at an awkward angle. Her chin thrust itself up into the air, as if it had a mind of its own.

Blood seeped from her eyes, ears and nose.

The SS automatically repeated the process a number of times, each time throwing the young girl's body into an ugly violent motion.

A green light flashed on the control panel.

Doctor Curr signalled for the nurses to undo the straps on the patient.

He sighed heavily as they casually went about their business. This is taking too long! It was supposed to be a holiday, he thought. What was he doing here? This convention was supposed to be his time-off! Damn! This is Hapsburg's job. He could be having a round of golf this afternoon.

Once again, the female nurse took too long to deliver the second injection.

Doctor Curr raced over, grabbed the needle and plunged it into the neck of the patient.

He waited.

The nurse waited.

The patient's chest didn't move.

Doctor Curr sighed heavily. He felt giddy when he tried to shake his head. Why? Why?

He looked at the nurse as she checked the pulse. She shook her head. The heart monitor showed no sign of life.

Doctor Curr pointed to the resuscitation equipment over in the corner, and stepped back to let them near the body.

The assistants moved quickly.

The body jerked violently at each application of electricity.

Nothing!

The chest remained motionless. Doctor Curr shook his head.

"Get her out of here!" he shouted in disgust.

Then he walked over to the film man and said in a low voice:

"We haven't got time to do another one. You'll have to edit this one so it looks like a successful therapy session. Can you do that?"

The film man nodded.

"Should be alright."

He adjusted his peculiar black and white cap to the back of his head and added:

"I took some film of the patient in the ward - before this. She had already been drugged but I think I can doctor it up to look like a successful therapy session."

Doctor Curr nodded and followed the nursing staff out of the ECT Unit. Time for a fix, he thought.

*

An auxiliary nurse remained behind, to clean up.

It was very quiet and she felt uneasy as she mopped away the blood from the face of the dead girl.

As she prepared the body for the morgue, she shook her head in dismay. Why does she always get the dirty jobs?

"Poor little thing," she whispered. "And to think I was speaking to you only minutes ago in your room. Your mother should be shot! Fancy not telling you about the facts of life and all that. How could she do this to you?"

She looked at the innocent face for a brief moment, then transferred the body to the portable bed.

The assistant nurse shook her head again. What was she doing in this place? This isn't the right job for her. If only the money wasn't so good. How many deaths had she seen now? She tried to recall them. There's something not quite right about this place. She thought about all the things she'd seen recently.

Psychiatric hospitals don't have to declare any of the deaths in their care. These dead people were now officially non-persons - especially when they were forced into psychiatric care and not admitted of their own free will. According to the records, they didn't exist. She had seen the files!

She once again looked down at the innocent face of the young girl.

A slight frown could be seen on her forehead.

A single tear trickled down her cheek.

She looked like she had just drifted off to sleep

The nurse looked around the ECT Unit and out through the door. No-one could be seen, so she bent down and listened for a heartbeat - just to be sure.

Nothing!

She covered the body and pushed the portable bed off towards the morgue.

"How did you end up in a place like this," she whispered to the body under the sheet.

"Come to think of it - how on earth did I end up in a place like this? If only the money wasn't so good. If only the money wasn't so good."

PART TWO

CHAPTER TWO

Darkness loomed over the bright lights of Sydney.

A crowd slowly moved from the foyer into the convention hall.

Psychiatrists from all over the planet milled about the huge hall, searching for or greeting long lost acquaintances.

Men in expensive black suits mingled with beautiful ladies glittering in their finest jewellery. Tables sparkled with lavish dinner settings, offset by dark red table covers. Chandeliers dimly glittered high above.

The Psychiatric Convention was about to begin.

The film man, in his peculiar black and white cap, sat in the middle of the hall. On the table in front of him rested the film projector - ready to go.

The most powerful people on the planet - psychiatrists, education authorities and other government ministers, drug manufacturers and media tycoons - laughed and chattered as they sat down.

He felt like he didn't belong and busied himself fiddling with his half-smoked cigarette.

'The Fiddler'! Yes! That's what they should call him, he mused.

He glanced at the film reel directly in front, on the table.

It wasn't the best splicing job he'd done but it should be good enough for this lot. After all - they'd be as drunk as skunks soon, or probably were already.

He looked around the great hall - a thousand, at least.

The noise level gradually increased until it became a continuous babble.

Then dinner was served. A long line of waiters scurried about tables serving up the rich and exotic foods. Spirits and wine, and then more spirits, followed.

The noise level went up in to another range! This time the clinking of glasses and clanking of cutlery joined in.

The film man didn't eat, but instead, satisfied his taste for good vodka.

A live orchestra played softly in the background, surely unheard by most of the guests.

Up on the stage - two to three feet above the main floor - the honoured dignitaries sat at a long table. The illustrious leaders of Psychiatry peered down at their colleagues.

Doctor Hapsburg, the Australian President, stood up and tapped the side of a glass with his spoon.

"Thank you," he said into the microphone.

The chatter continued.

"Thank you, Ladies and Gentlemen," he said louder.

The chatter, if anything, increased.

"Silence!" he shouted.

Everyone hushed, except the usual few gigglers who never obey such a request wherever they are.

When he finally achieved complete silence, all the men up on the front table pushed their chairs back and stood to face the convention majority.

Then the delegates rose from their seats to join their leaders.

The film man reluctantly followed suit, not wanting to attract undue attention.

Everyone lifted their glasses and yelled:

"Hail Psychiatry!"

Some could be heard clicking their heels.

Then they all sat down except for Doctor Hapsburg. He squinted as the strong spotlights zoomed in on him.

He cleared his throat before beginning.

"Good evening Ladies and Gentlemen. I hope you enjoyed the food. Despite the rumours about the American laser infiltration, the conference will go ahead as originally planned."

Murmurs and whispers interrupted the Doctor's opening address. The majority of the hall looked at the ceiling. Some pointed up while explaining the satellite listening system to the person next to them.

"Silence!" continued Doctor Hapsburg. "We have a lot to do tonight so I shall be as brief as possible." The crowd hushed and gave their attention to the front once more.

"Ladies and Gentlemen, - the days of National Pride are over, and I do not think any of us regret their passing. The old ideas of National Folk Heroes and Culture have given way to the much finer ideal of The United States of the Supreme Fatherland of Germany. The ties that now bind us together are less obvious but far stronger than before, because they rest on sounder foundations.

"We have much to be proud of in the achievements of Psychiatry, first founded in Germany; but our greatest pride must surely be in the way it has developed into the planetary power it is today.

"It is an example to the world of how free, democratic peoples, separated from one another by many thousands of miles, can live together in voluntary association brought about by Psychiatry's policies. The efficient use of generous handouts from governments so that Psychiatry could carry out these policies is not to be overlooked.

"The solidarity of this unification of nations under the banner of the Supreme Fatherland has twice been sorely tested of recent times, and on each occasion it has become stronger.

"At the turn of the century in the 1900's, some two hundred years ago, we, of the Supreme Fatherland, used to call ourselves 'The Brain Theory Troops', and we were at first puzzled when ancient cultures described us as 'Oddballs' or 'The Brain Theory Cult'.

"In our overwhelming belief, it had not occurred to us that people of the ancient spiritual cultures would oppose us so violently.

"The achievements of Psychiatry's fighting few from the past need no fresh praise from me now. They are too well known, and have taken an honoured place in history.

"Little good comes out of the evils of spiritual cultures. But those of us who are privileged to have ancestors who served alongside great leaders of the past who supported our 'Brain Theory', and those who crusaded up through the ages will never be forgotten.

"I do not need to remind you how 'The Brain Theory' has withstood the test of time, in our happier days of peace.

"When the Supreme Fatherland entered the long struggle for supremacy, it was Psychiatry and their mental hospitals that were the first to give the help that was needed so badly.

"Then later again, it was the Psychiatrists who sent electric shock machines and mind-enhancing drugs such as LSD into societies where they were needed so badly - not out of any deluded thought for the spirit but only for the purpose of healing brains. This was how the Supreme Fatherland was able to win the fight.

"Vast sums of money were allocated to Psychiatry during these battles, and through force of necessity, the German people rationed themselves simply in order to help win the war. We shall never forget this.

"National pride and ancient cultures that have survived long periods of time, are accused of paying too much attention to the illusion of spiritual values.

"We of the Supreme Fatherland recognised the fault, and I think I am right in saying that our Australian colleagues now also realise this illusion.

"Even though the Australian heritage is not long in the making, you should rightly be proud of your contribution and the gigantic steps taken towards future betterment.

"If 'The Brain Theory' can replace national pride and deluded spiritual teachings, and from now on, mean as much to your people as it does to ours, then it is a very vital theory indeed. Its true significance goes far beyond national pride and spiritual delusions.

"To Psychiatry it means not only control and strength in unification, but a united ideal across the whole planet. Psychiatry has developed the means to achieve this - the electric shock machine, brain drugs, hospitalisation and treatment of revolutionaries, and then a complete re-education of the entire population of Earth.

"In closing, I would like to add a special thanks to governments around the world, especially the Australian politicians here tonight. What causes our admiration most is the total support given to us by these Members of Parliament. With their financial assistance and help in revising current laws, the aims of Psychiatry will be achieved.

"Ladies and Gentlemen, I give the toast, on behalf of world-wide Psychiatry, to the International President of Psychiatry - Doctor Hanover!"

People jumped to their feet. Applause echoed around the huge hall.

Doctor Hanover graciously accepted the standing ovation and toast.

He adjusted his white suit and mopped at his perspiring forehead. When the applause died, he took a few moments to gather his thoughts and let people return to their seats.

He carefully groomed his little black bushy moustache and then stood up. Squinting into the powerful spotlights he said:

"Ladies and Gentlemen - I am very happy to reply on behalf of Psychiatry to the generous welcome you have given to this toast. Flattering things have been said about us, and I am almost tempted to say that I wouldn't have the heart to ask you to denounce Australia as an independent country, because of my own deep regard for the Fatherland.

"But you know that it is the greatest good for the greatest number that should only ever concern us. You also know that Psychiatrists don't have hearts, only cold and calculating brains. And you also know it will be to everyone's advantage, so I propose that you keep your country's name only, but be officially recognised as a southern state of the Supreme Fatherland of Germany. And may I add that there will be generous benefits bestowed upon those who help to bring about this alliance.

"Among us are distinguished representatives of the government, drug companies, television and newspaper media. Hand in hand, all of us will reap the rewards and profits of such an historic unification. As the official ambassador from the USSF of Germany, you have my word that money will flow to those hands that help build this alliance.

"Of course there are some small obstacles that must be cleared from our path. With your help, I am positive these will be quickly dealt with.

"Ladies and Gentlemen, - Thank you for your support."

A standing ovation kept Doctor Hanover from getting in a final word.

Eventually, when the audience settled back into their seats, he continued.

"Now let's get on with the entertainment. But first, very briefly, Doctor Hapsburg has a little surprise for you."

The film man took his cue. He waited for Doctor Hapsburg to signal.

Doctor Hapsburg stood up once more and addressed the audience.

Music blasted out of gigantic speakers, multicoloured lights flashed across the stage and a drum roll brought the conference to its feet once more.

"Ladies and gentlemen, the new wonder drugs, Riddalem and Prozad, will now be available through prescription to all the states of the Fatherland. With laws passed, we now have school children, the aged in nursing homes, the disabled, the mentally ill and most of the society's needy on these drugs.

"With new laws about to be passed, we will also soon have the middle-age bracket seeking psychiatric drugs as well."

Huge banners slowly descended down the wall behind the Doctor. Full-length pictures of the latest drugs' advertising campaigns covered the entire stage.

The conference applauded continuously.

"But that's only the tip of the iceberg!

"Ladies and Gentlemen, I now have the honour in announcing the release of the latest and most advanced technology in the field of mental health!

"I proudly give you 'The Super Seven Shocker', the culmination of the hardest struggle over many years battling against Human Rights Groups. This latest state of the art ECT machine will bring glory to the Fatherland!"

An assistant wheeled the SS out onto the centre of the stage. It gleamed and sparkled in the spotlights.

The film man started up the projector and waited.

The audience went wild!

After what seemed like ages Doctor Hapsburg finally got the chance to continue.

" And that's not all. Ladies and Gentlemen, tonight we have a special treat for you. Tonight you will see the Super Seven at work before your very own eyes."

He pointed to an assistant and a full length white screen descended at the side of the stage. Then he gave the cue to the film man.

As the projector beamed toward the screen, all the lights in the convention hall were lowered, spreading darkness across the massive room.

Colour flashed onto the screen and then the young girl appeared. Her long silky hair gave an image of innocence and purity. Her white gown added the effect of angelic beauty as she lay on the hospital bed.

The film rolled on without a hitch.

Not a bad splicing job, thought the film man. A real pro would see straight through the phoney set-up but it's good enough for this bunch of amateurs.

Just as he finished praising his own workmanship, the projector gave out a loud clunk.

"Hold on!" he mumbled. "Not now! Come on!"

The film stuck on the very last frame - a shot of the girl. She sat up in bed with a silly grin on her face. Footage from before the afternoon's ECT fiasco had been spliced in at the end to make it appear like a successful therapy session.

There was one major problem with that very last frame. The film man had only been able to get one shot of the girl smiling. And that had been for a brief few seconds after the administering of the pre-operation drugs.

The smile was abnormal. There was definitely something unsettling about the lifeless eyes and crooked mouth of the patient.

It had been planned that the last frame would stay on the screen for only a couple of seconds. Before any of the keener members of the audience could spot the outpoint, the film was supposed to change to a shot of a white dove flying off into the distance and then the words: THE END.

The film man frantically pressed buttons, pulled at the reels and tried everything to get it unstuck.

It was no use!

Luckily, the majority of the audience stood applauding, whooping and hollering. They were none the wiser.

"Hail Psychiatry!" some called out above the general noise. Doctor Curr, sitting on the end of the main table up on the stage, and the only other person to know about the phoney set-up, glared at the film man.

Doctor Curr's head shot back and forth from the screen to the projector, all the while signalling to turn it off.

The film man eventually found the power cable plug in the dark and pulled it apart. The screen went black.

Doctor Hapsburg, unaware, resumed the duties of chairman. Broadly smiling and applauding the SS - seated beside the table - he went on to say:

"Thank you Ladies and gentlemen, and now for some entertainment. Please put your hands together for the biggest show business act to come out of the Supreme Fatherland since the Dancing Bears of Bosnia! Yes, Ladies and Gentlemen, none other than The Transvestite Psycho Tropics!"

Adult males, with effeminate bodies, cat-walked out onto the stage. They were dressed in typical dancing-girl show costumes with plumes of feathers and all the usual frills.

False breasts were rubbed on the faces of the honoured Doctors of Psychiatry, still sitting at their table up on the stage.

One by one the frills were removed. The crowd cried out, urging them to get their gear off.

The film man packed up his equipment and decided to leave early. Not a good night, he thought. Not a good week, more like it!

Out in the lobby, things were so quiet he stopped for a moment to adjust to the sudden change from the noise inside. When he felt relaxed, he tucked the film case up under his arm, lit a cigarette and headed out the front doors.

"Uh oh!" he stopped in his tracks as a teenage girl stuck her face in front of his.

She held a placard high and screamed into his face.

"Psychiatry Killers!

"Psychiatry Killers!

"Nazi Murderers!

"Nazi Murderers!"

Other protesters circled him and joined the girl's taunts.

The film man made a dash for it. He broke through the ring and ran down the footpath. Quickly he pulled his tell-tale black and white cap from his head and tried to lose himself in the crowd.

"I need another drink," he mumbled. When the coast looked clear he headed for the nearest bar.

Perched on a seat, and with two glasses of vodka already downed, he let out a stream of blue cigarette smoke in relief.

Then he finished off another vodka and sighed.

"There's got to be an easier way to make a quid."

The barman put another vodka in front of him and took his money.

"There's got to be an easier way," he repeated. "If only the money wasn't so good." The film man shook his head and lit another cigarette.

"If only the damn money wasn't so good!"

PART TWO

CHAPTER THREE

Alma stood in the early morning glow of the desert.

She looked back at the secret entrance to the caves for a brief moment. Was it a good idea or not? Invisible forces pulled at her to go back to the safety of the rebels. She fought them off.

It was impossible to change her mind now. She just had to make the journey. It would be hell living with herself if she didn't go to Sydney.

There wasn't even a good reason for going, she attempted to argue. No! It had to be done. It was a once in a life time chance.

The silence of the desert made her feel lonely.

Alma quickly shrugged off the negative thoughts and started walking south towards Broken Hill. She imagined the others down in the cave still sleeping soundly next to their fires.

Someone yelled from behind.

"Hey! Hold up a minute!"

Two dark figures came up out of the ground.

It was Nulla and Darcy! They wore nothing except string around their wastes and bands around their heads. In their hands were spears and boomerangs. Darcy also had a throwing stick.

Alma waited anxiously as they strolled towards her. Nulla didn't smile.

"My grandfather, the tribal elder, told us to come after you," he said

Alma dug her toes into the hot sand - ready to resist.

Darcy laughed at her and then looked at Nulla.

"And take you as far as Bourke, over in the east," he continued. "Then you're on your own."

Before Alma could protest that she didn't expect them to risk their lives for her, both men had walked off into the morning sun.

By the time she had caught up with the two warriors she realised that Old George was right - she did need their help, at least in that part of the unknown desert. And going east instead of south would be safer.

Many days later the three travellers reached the outskirts of Bourke. They had walked east, away from the security of the secret caves; then past the electric fence to the north end of the compound; and over the great flat desert plains.

Alma had marvelled at the massive salt lakes. They stopped and looked at unusual paintings under small outcrops of rocks. They crossed dry creek beds, that looked like they were carved from the wanderings of giant snakes. The leaps and bounds of the kangaroos made her laugh. Curious emus gracefully approached her as she stood and watched them. Rabbits, dingoes, foxes, lizards and birds of every size crossed their path.

Alma had almost forgotten about going to the city.

Nulla had kept his distance and spoke the bare minimum when she tried to make friends. It was too late to try now - especially after she had given him the cold shoulder earlier in the secret caves.

Darcy had been his usual carefree self and had broken the ice, many times, during their long walk.

A man-made road lay before them. The blue-stone gravel road stretched out across the desert sands to disappear amongst the mulga bush.

They followed it for a short time and came upon a car and caravan parked at the side of the gravel. After watching the people for some time, two adults and two young girls, Nulla decided it was worth a try and sent Alma forward.

She glanced back at her two friends hiding behind trees, then reluctantly approached the family.

The younger of the girls spotted Alma and yelled to her mother. The family stopped eating and stared.

The father wiped his hands on his khaki shorts, slowly stood up and warily walked towards her.

He stroked his short black hair as he surveyed the surrounding desert for signs of others.

"Yes?" he said, still searching the trees for others.

Alma hesitated. She wanted to run away but something inside told her it would be alright if she stayed at a distance for the moment. She pulled at the hem of her white summer frock and adjusted the shoulder strap of her bag.

She tried to think, and could only manage to stare. What do I say? I should have thought of something first. Now I'm standing here like some sort of idiot.

"Hi!" It was the only thing she could think of to say.

"Are you alright?" said the father. "Has there been some sort of trouble?"

"I'm going to Sydney. Could you give me a ride, please?"

The father looked at the family. The woman nodded her head.

"Come and have a cuppa. You can tell us what's happened," said the woman. She brushed the flies from her face and the ants from her blue and white frock.

"Damn ants!" said the young mother. "The flies are bad enough without having to put up with these little pests too."

Within the hour the car and caravan pulled away from the parking bay. Alma and the two young girls sat in the caravan as it jolted and jerked its way along behind the car.

Alma suddenly realised she had forgotten something and dived for the back window.

As she pushed the curtain to the side, two black figures could be seen far off in the distance.

The car gathered speed and the caravan swayed from side to side.

Nulla and Darcy gradually shrunk in the distance as the car went further. One of them could be seen walking off to the side of the road.

A lone black figure, standing in the middle of the road, getting further and further away, lifted a spear into the air and waved after her.

As he disappeared in the shimmering heat waves, Alma burst into uncontrollable fits of sobbing. Tears streamed down her face. She frantically waved her hands but it was too late - he had disappeared from her life.

She knew it was Nulla. It was Nulla who had stayed and waved - not Darcy. She just knew it.

What am I doing? I must be crazy!

152

Alma peered out the back window for along time before she eventually pulled herself together.

Then her attention fell on the back curtain. When she closed it, the sun shone through the thin cloth to show a dark blue background with a white diagonal cross.

"That's our national flag," said the eldest girl, about ten years of age. "Do you want to play 'Doctors and Nurses'?'"

Alma moved along the bed, closer to the girls.

"Ellie can be the patient; and you can be the nurse; and I'll be the doctor. OK?"

"I want to be the nurse," complained Ellie.

"If you don't be the patient, we won't let you play. Isn't that right Alma?"

"It's alright Molly. I'll be the patient." She looked back at the flag. "What country do you come from?"

"Scotland," said Molly. "My dad says that Germany is trying to take our country from us but we won't let them. You should come and stay with us after we go home. We've got a king, and a castle, and the Highlands, and the Loch Ness Monster, but no-one has seen Nessy yet. You would really like it. Will you come?"

"I don't know if I could. I have to do something else first and I don't know how long that will take. But if I get a chance I will."

"Alright! Now, you lie down on the bed and pretend you're dying."

Alma lay on the bed and closed her eyes. The caravan dipped and swayed as it sped along the road.

After some time it slowed down. All three peered out the windows. They passed a sign at the side of the road.

'Gulargonbone. Population 201'

Within minutes they were parked in front of the town café.

Stepping out into the bright sunlight, Alma was glad to have a spell from the hot cramped space of the little caravan.

Everyone had a good stretch before approaching the café.

Three young men - barefoot - sat against the wall of the old wooden building, under the shade of the veranda.

"Afternoon!" said the father. "There wouldn't be a laundry-mat in this place, would there?"

The red haired youth looked at the other two, laughed and then slowly looked down one end of the road before turning to the other end.

Alma followed his gaze.

Half a dozen old buildings and a hotel stood here and there. Small houses shaded by trees were scattered further off in the distance.

"You a Pom?" said another youth, tipping his hat back.

"A Pom is an Englishman. I'm a Scotsman," said the father.

"What's a Scotsman?"

"It's someone who comes from Scotland."

"And where the hell is that?" added the red haired youth.

"Up near the North Pole," said the father.

"Up nearrrr the Norrrth Pole" mimicked the third youth, rolling his r's. All three laughed and the Scottish father laughed with them.

He then interrupted their teasing.

"I'll bet at least two of you young laddies have Scottish blood in you're veins."

"Well what do you know!" said the red haired youth, putting on a show of surprise. "Did you hear that, Rom? Scottish blood, he says."

"Scottish blood, my eye!" said the youth with the hat.

"You lassies go in and get a drink," said the father.

As the girls walked through the door, the red haired youth looked Alma up and down.

"And what about that one in the white dress?" he said. "She from Scotland too?"

"Aye. Could even be a distance cousin of yours," laughed the father.

As Alma walked into the café she heard the reply.

"I think you been out in the sun too long, Pom." All three laughed and the red head continued. "Oh yeah! If you want a laundry-mat in this dead-end place, better come back in about a hundred years and maybe - just maybe - you might be lucky enough to find one."

The father joined the others inside the cafe as the youths laughed at the future prospect.

He looked over towards Alma and gave her a wink and a smile.

With their thirsts quenched and a short rest in the café, it was time to move on.

Alma peered out the caravan window as they approached the outskirts of Gulargonbone. A small school building hid under the shade of a huge eucalyptus tree. Children screamed and ran around the yard.

The school whizzed passed them. She wondered about the children - what would it be like growing up in a small town such as this? At least there wouldn't be any electric fences! Could this small town have had Blacks living in it at one time? Of course! We lived all over Australia along time ago, she thought. Now, it's just the compounds. Why did they call the compounds 'Australwitz One' and 'Australwitz Two'?

Thoughts ran through her mind at an ever-increasing speed now.

She had passed through the bigger town of Bourke and smaller towns such as Gulargonbone. As they continued south-east, the towns grew in size.

Alma looked at the two young girls playing next to her in the caravan. She couldn't help wondering how it was that most white people were so alike - it was hard to distinguish one from another because of their similar features.

Did they also think that all Blacks looked the same? She had only ever seen two Whites - that is, before meeting this Scottish family.

It was the first real lie she had ever told - that she was an American, on holidays. That she had been hitch-hiking around Australia, with friends, but had found it too difficult and decided to return to her relations in Sydney.

It would be the first of many lies to be told if she was to see Sydney without getting caught. No-one was going to send her back to the compound and that crazy hospital. She would say anything to make sure that that never happened.

Anxious as Alma was about the city, the dark cloud of the compound gradually lifted from her eyes the more they travelled south.

New towns and tall buildings passed by.

Butterflies whirled around inside her stomach when the car eventually stopped on the outskirts of Sydney.

"This is as far as we can take you Alma," said the Scotsman. "We're taking the By-pass to Canberra."

She shook hands with everyone and stood at the side of the road as the car continued on its journey.

"Don't forget to visit us in Scotland," screamed Molly, leaning out the window.

It was too late for Alma to reply - the car sped off down the road.

She waved goodbye.

At the city boundary stood a massive stone wall, at least twenty feet high, that disappeared off into the distance in both directions.

Signs were posted all over the place:

'Off Limits To Fuel Burning Vehicles - $50,000 Fine'

'Pollution Free Zone'

'No Weapons - $20,000 Fine'

'Welcome To Sydney'

Trucks loaded cargo through wide doors in the wall that ran the full length in either direction.

As Alma walked in through the entrance gate for pedestrians, crowds of people gathered on many platforms. Trains and trams and buses filled the huge domed terminal. Bargain prices covered the walls.

A sign caught her attention.

'City Centre Express'

She cautiously stepped aboard the sleek train.

Seated in the most comfortable cushioned armchair she had ever experienced, Alma stared out the window at the moving platform. It was as if the platform, full of people, slowly and silently moved backwards away from the train. The train seemed to remain where it was!

Soon her eyes adjusted to the illusion. And the train rocketed through the suburbs, gathering speed all the while.

The clear aquamarine sky was a complete contrast to the pale blue of the desert. Puffs of pure white clouds were scattered here and there. Buildings tried to reach up to the clouds. Massive mirror-like windows completely covered the skyscrapers and reflected images of clouds down into Alma's compartment.

So many buildings tightly packed together! How could people live like this? She wondered if every city was the same.

All of a sudden everything went absolutely black. The train continued to rattle on through the darkness. Lights lit up a sign as the train slowed.

'CITY CENTRE'

Pushed by the crowd, Alma soon found herself off the train and flowing along as if a part of a stream - unable to stop. Down this tunnel, up that platform, riding to a higher level by automatic moving-stairs, pushed along further tunnels until she finally arrived up into the bright light of the day once more.

The crowd from the train joined hundreds more rushing along the streets. In desperation she ducked to the side and hugged the safety of a small tree on the edge of the footpath.

Funny shaped cars silently raced up and down the roads.

Lights flashed orange, red and green.

When Alma felt that she had soaked in enough of the strange surroundings, she rejoined the crowd and flowed along some more.

A long wide motorway stretched out ahead and ended at the top of a hill far off into the distance. On top of the hill sat a magnificent building. And on top of the building flashed a giant multi-coloured sign.

'KINGS CROSS HOTEL'

She kept her eye on it as she walked towards it. The crowd thinned and made it easier to take in the sights.

The sun was past noon now.

Alma pulled out the crunched-up money from her bag. Old George had given it to Nulla, who had passed it on to her.

Her stomach rumbled.

A group of people walked into a tall building just up ahead so she followed them.

All sorts of weird things startled her as she walked along the main corridor - automatic doors, moving statues, dancers and singers glittering in costumes, overhead screens with musicians blasting out tunes and much more.

Many times her eyes darted in disbelief and many times her heart jumped into her mouth.

This building, she thought, was a city within a city!

Eventually the smell of food caught her attention.

Inside a shop she mimicked others and ordered a 'number one'.

A blonde-haired youth joined Alma at a table, pulled out some tobacco and offered it to her.

She shook her head.

"Where are you from?" he said.

"America."

"So am I. What part?"

"India, first. Then I moved to America later." Alma tried to smile at ease but could feel the tension showing itself.

"That explains the accent," said the youth. He lit up the cigarette and went on:

"I can't believe the prices here in Australia. And then on top of that you get stung with income tax and sales tax. The beauty of the USSF of A, is no taxes!"

Alma smiled a half smile and turned to stare out the window, wanting desperately to be left alone.

A man in a grey suit and hat stared back at her from the other side of the main walkway. She suddenly felt trapped. The whole experience overwhelmed her and now someone was staring at her. Why? Quickly gathering up her bag she headed for the door. The man in the grey suit followed her.

"Hey! Stop!" he yelled.

Alma walked faster, towards the exit.

The man was running now.

Alma quickened her pace.

He had nearly caught up with her - only yards from her.

Then, right at the last instant a boy dashed past her and out through the main doors into the street.

An old woman screamed.

"My bag! My bag! He's got my bag!"

Alma ran out through the main doors. The man in the grey suit rushed past her. As he did so, he called back to her:

"You wait there. I want to talk to you."

He pulled out something from his pocket and yelled into it as he chased after the boy.

Alma waited a second or two, then decided to make a run for it. She turned and ran in the opposite direction to the one taken by the man in the grey suit.

Soon she was at the top of the road, standing in front of the Kings Cross Hotel. Gasping for air, she mingled with a crowd walking up a street to the left.

A sign jutted out of the side of a building. 'Public Toilet.'

Alma ducked inside, hid in one of the cubicles and locked the door. She tried to calm herself down by taking long slow breaths.

A group of girls walked in, noisily chatting to one another. This put her at ease slightly. They talked of boys and where would be the next best place to go shopping.

Alma worked up enough courage to leave the cubicle after changing into shorts and t-shirt.

Two black girls talking to two white girls, took her by surprise. They brushed their hair and giggled at each other in the mirror.

They didn't look like her kind, but would have been roughly the same age as Alma. One had streaks of blonde in her otherwise natural black hair. The other had long, plaited natural black hair - almost as long as Alma's.

The two white girls spoke the same accent as Alma but the two black girls spoke like the blonde-haired youth in the food shop earlier. They could only be Americans, she thought.

Alma brushed her own hair and listened in.

The more she secretly watched them, the more she decided that they didn't look that much different in physique. From this Alma became more confident of passing herself off as an American - just as long as she kept her mouth shut, no-one would be the wiser.

"Let's go see a movie," said a white girl.

"No. The boys are going to take us for a ride. Come on, let's go! They're waiting for us," said the American with black hair.

The American with the streaky blonde-black hair laughed at her.

"You got one thing on your mind girl. Come on Lemmy, leave the boys alone for awhile. They'll still be there when we get out of the movies."

"Would you just listen to my big sister. The girl that said she was going to let it all hang out on her holidays. You 'come on' yourself Atty, we can see all the movies we want when we get back home. I'm here to have some fun. And my man is out there waiting for me in his big black car. I'm going. See you all back at the hostel later."

The girl called Lemmy walked out with the other three following and still pleading.

The streaky blonde American, the one they called Atty, turned at the last moment to catch Alma staring at her, and gave her a smile before she left.

Curious of their wild clothes, carefree attitude and freedom to do as they pleased in Australia, she felt drawn towards them.

By the time Alma had walked outside, the car - loaded with girls and boys - was already moving off down the road.

Without thinking, she walked along the footpath in the same direction.

Men called to her from shop doorways.

"Come in and see the show, darling."

"How much, sweetheart?"

"Step right up and see the greatest strip-show on Earth."

"Free entry for women. Full strip and double acts!"

"All you can drink for five dollars and dance your socks off till 5 AM."

From one end of the street to the other and back down the other side as well - it was all the same, over and over again.

Dusk spread across the sky.

A sign just inside an alley-way caught her attention.

'Rooms To Rent'

She walked into a dark doorway, up dimly lit stairs and into the reception area.

"Overnight or longer?" said an old woman hidden behind the counter.

"Single or share?" she continued.

When Alma didn't answer, the old woman peered over the top, blew out a stream of blue smoke and said in a croaky voice:

"Well?"

"Do you have a room I could rent tonight?"

"Fifteen dollars plus tax," croaked the old woman.

Alma passed over the crinkled-up money. The old woman inspected the notes for a long time and then looked at Alma.

Eventually, she handed her a key and said:

"401. Fourth floor. Be out by 9 AM. Showers are at the end of the corridor."

The high-pressure shower was a novelty. Bathing at the compound didn't come close to this - a five-minute walk to the main canal; a short swim and that was that! Alma wanted to stay under the hot water forever. It felt so relaxing as the jets of water massaged her head, neck and body.

Sitting at the single-bedroom window, she could see the flashing coloured lights above the shops and hear the voices, of the crowds, drifting up from below.

An occasional scream could be heard far off into the distance.

All of a sudden the loneliness of the room hit her. The atmosphere just didn't feel right - there was something cold and impersonal about it.

Tired and exhausted from all that she had seen that day, she lay on the bed and let her heavy eyelids close.

As tired as she was, her mind raced from one scene to another.

The man in the grey suit kept pushing his way into her mind. Did he recognise that she was from the compound? Or did he want her for something else? Finally the outside noise drifted away and she fell asleep.

With no clock to tell the time, Alma left the building early the next morning.

The street was deserted except for a noisy truck and two men sweeping up the mountains of rubbish.

A Breakfast Bar, just two doors down, caught her attention.

Inside, were the two Americans - sitting at the only table - eating breakfast.

She suddenly stopped halfway through the door. Were they about to discover her secret? If she stayed, she would have to open her mouth. Before Alma could turn to leave, the blonde-black American was speaking to her.

"Hi! You can share our table, if you like."

Alma smiled and automatically sat down.

"Are you just visiting or do you live here?"

"Visiting," said Alma.

"I'm Atlanta but they call me Atty. This is my darling little sister - Lemmy. Her real name is Lemuria."

Atty waited for Alma to give her name.

"Well? Are you going to tell us yours or is it a state secret?"

Both girls laughed at each other.

"Alma."

"The coffee isn't too bad but I wouldn't recommend anything else."

Alma smiled, stood up, ordered a coffee from the girl behind the counter, and rejoined the Americans at the table.

"Don't worry about Lemmy. She has a hangover. You'll be lucky to get any sense out of her before the middle of the day."

Lemmy laughed and rubbed at her eyes, hidden by a pair of dark sunglasses.

"I might have a hangover but I wouldn't have missed last night for all the gold in Fort Knox."

"You on holidays too?" said Atty.

"Sort of." Alma sipped at her coffee.

"Where do you come from?"

"India."

Atty and Lemmy looked at each other and burst out laughing.

Alma could feel her cheeks heating up and beginning to glow.

"Well, I wasn't born there. I moved there later," said Alma.

"Where from?" Atty said. Lemmy just smiled, rubbed her forehead occasionally and sipped at her coffee.

"New Zealand." Alma suddenly realised that she wasn't a very convincing liar. She should've worked all this out before coming to Sydney.

"It's OK. You can tell us any story you like. But I have to warn you - we've been travelling around the world for some time now and you aren't from India or New Zealand. Mind you - I'm no expert, but at a rough guess, I'd say you are Australian. What do you think, Lemmy?"

Lemmy shrugged her shoulders, deciding to stay out of it.

"I'm not trying to give you a hard time Alma but in case you haven't noticed, we are black as well. The Whites think we all look the same, but as the Australians say - you can't pull the wool over our eyes.

"Well, maybe over Lemmy's eyes this morning - but not mine."

Atty laughed at both of them.

Alma began to feel annoyed with herself - for lying in the first place and then being found out so easily.

"I think I better go," she said.

As Alma stood up, Atty grabbed her by the arm.

"Hey! It's alright. We don't care where you come from. I was only having a little bit of fun. I'm sorry."

Alma smiled and headed for the door.

"Now look what you've gone and done, you big bully," said Lemmy. "Hey Alma! Don't worry about her."

Alma turned and smiled to show that she had no bad feelings about them. Before she made it through the door Atty spoke again.

"Yeah! Come on back and finish your coffee. We're going for a swim after this - down at the beach. Why don't you come with us."

Alma smiled again and then shook her head before leaving.

After walking a few paces down the footpath she stopped, looked at the concrete below her sandals for a couple of seconds, and whispered.

"They'd keep my secret. And anyway - with a quick change of clothes, a pair of sunglasses, and, hanging around two other black girls - who would be able to tell her apart from the Americans?"

She turned and went back to finish her coffee.

By the time breakfast was finished Alma had told her story - with a lot of interrogation from the American sisters.

Atty finished her coffee, stood up and said:

"We'll go back to the room and get you a swimming costume."

"America is the land of plenty," said Lemmy, drumming her fingers on the table.

Alma looked at her and wondered what she meant.

Atty also gave Lemmy a look. And when it was obvious that her sister didn't intend to elaborate on the short statement, she asked:

"Just what are you working on, girl?"

"If I was in Alma's trouble, and if I were Alma, I would let my hair all the way down. If I were Alma I'd go to America for a holiday. You know! Before going back to the caves to live for the rest of my life, I'd shoot for the highest star," said Lemmy. Her eyes were hidden behind black sunglasses but a cheeky smile lingered on her pink lips.

Atty glanced from Lemmy to Alma.

Alma glanced from Lemmy to Atty.

The two Americans burst out laughing at the same time.

Alma smiled but didn't quite understand what they had in mind.

PART   TWO

CHAPTER   FOUR

Alma looked all around the vast space of the airport terminal.

Crowds of people jostled their way through other crowds of people, all going in different directions. It appeared to be complete chaos, but Lemmy and Atty didn't seem too worried.

The building would have easily matched the size of the main cave out in the desert.

Alma listened as Lemmy attempted to put her at ease once again.

"Just walk like we showed you. Don't panic and if any-one speaks to you, just nod your head, then keep walking." Lemmy thought that it was a great joke - holding her hand to her mouth to stop the giggles.

Alma managed a smile. She didn't feel at all comfortable in Lemmy's tight skirt, low cut top, sunglasses and plaited hair.

Atty didn't help matters either. She slapped Alma on the back and laughed at her appearance.

"You'll be alright girl. Just do what I said - follow me, and don't speak. Let me do the talking if anyone says anything."

Alma nodded.

Lemmy kissed Alma and Atty, waved goodbye and grabbed her Aussie boyfriend's arm. As she walked away snuggling into him, Atty called after her:

"Two weeks. No more! I'll ring to let you know what day Alma will be coming back. Remember Lemmy - two weeks only."

Lemmy waved a casual hand at her without looking back.

She disappeared into the crowd with her new boyfriend.

Alma moved in closer to Atty for support. She clutched at Lemmy's passport and papers. She was as good as Atty's little sister now.

They stepped onto the conveyor-belt walkway. As they neared the immigration officials at their check-points, the butterflies in her stomach spread out over her whole body. Her hands and legs shook uncontrollably.

Atty grabbed the passport from her hand, opened it and placed it next to her own on the counter as they passed the check-point.

The official didn't even bother to look at either of them. A machine sucked in the passports, made a strange noise and spat them back out onto the counter where Atty casually collected them.

She turned and smiled as she returned Lemmy's passport to Alma.

"There you go! Nothing to it!"

The conveyor carried them to a passenger waiting room.

Another ten minutes, thought Alma, and I'll be on an Air Rocket to the USSF of America. Surely this must be a dream. She looked down at the multi-coloured short skirt that Lemmy had insisted she wear. No - it couldn't be a dream.

"Flight 0T2102 boarding," came the call from an overhead speaker.

"That's us," smiled Atty.

Once they were aboard, Alma thought her jitters would fade away.

But it was as if the butterflies in her stomach had found a new higher level of agitation.

Everything about the Air Rocket was completely beyond her wildest dreams. The walls, ceiling and floor were transparent, and were made up of a honeycomb pattern of hundreds of little six-sided widows.

Down below, passengers on the lower deck could be seen getting in to their seats. Up above, more passengers on the higher deck walked along the transparent walkway searching for their seats.

It was like looking out of a glass beehive.

There must've been anywhere up to five hundred people on each of the three levels.

Other planes - apart from these American Air Rockets - were of the old style. Alma had seen pictures of them back in her school days at the compound. But these newer American models gave her the feeling of being on another planet.

A high pitched bell-like noise brought her attention to the front.

A speaker burbled out lists of numbers and speeds and heights.

Without warning the Air Rocket lifted up into the air. It hovered silently for a few seconds before hurtling straight up into the sky.

Atty, sitting beside her, turned and laughed at the expression on Alma's face.

Alma knew that she must look silly but the experience was so wonderful that she just didn't care what any-one thought about her.

Atty threw her streaked hair back over the top of her seat and relaxed.

She then pressed some buttons on the arm-rest beside her. A white screen shot out of the end section and unfolded in front of her lap. When more buttons were pressed, a colour picture appeared. As Atty adjusted earphones and pressed more buttons, people appeared on the screen.

Atty then started speaking to the people on the screen! And, they spoke back to her - as if they could see her!

In what felt like a very short time, they were landing in Denver - somewhere in the middle of America.

"There you go, Alma!" laughed Atty. "I bet your friends back in the caves are worrying about you surviving in the big city of Sydney. And here you are! Too bad you can't send them a postcard, hey?"

Atty laughed so much that Alma couldn't help but join in.

"Come on, girl," she eventually said. "Just a short trip now and we'll be home. You'll love Castle Rock, it's not far from here. It's a beautiful little place."

Atty threw their bags into a strange looking car. It didn't have a driver or any wheels! Once inside, she pushed a small plastic card into a slot and tapped some buttons.

"Put that strap across your waist," she said.

The car then rose up into the air and, like the Air Rocket, hovered briefly before shooting off up into the sky.

Below them the land passed by as a blur, as they flew south.

Soon they were unloading their bags out the front of Atty's house.

The car took off, up into the sky again, without a driver, and headed back toward the direction they had come from.

"Well, here it is! Home sweet home." Atty motioned for Alma to follow her as she walked up the steps onto the front porch. "Oh! It's good to be home. I'd definitely do a world trip again, next week even, but there's no place like home."

Compared to the tin huts in the compound and the timber houses she had seen in Australia, these American stone houses were massive. The sun shining on the white walls dazzled Alma's eyes.

"That's Lemmy's bedroom in there," said Atty. "Make yourself at home. It's yours for two weeks, use anything you like."

Atty disappeared for a few minutes then returned.

"I'm going to have a shower and a sleep. Kitchen is down the end of the hall. I'll leave you to find your way around the rest of the place."

"Thanks Atty. It's a beautiful house. It's so big! And you say that just the two of you live here?" Alma sat on the bed, looking at all the wonderful things that Lemmy had decorated her room with.

"Our daddy is very rich. Our parents stay here when they're not travelling to some far away place for holidays. It's too bad you won't get to taste mama's cooking - maybe next time, hey?"

"I think I could do with a rest too. So much has happened in the last few days. It'll take me weeks to catch up."

"Alma, I think you could take on the whole world.

"Not many people would've had the guts to do what you have done, and not many people would've bounced back as you have - especially after what those cowards did in the desert. You're a fighter!" Atty laughed. "But even heavy-weight fighters need a rest. I'll see you ... I'll see you whenever you get up."

The two girls looked at each other briefly and smiled. Then Atty walked off down the hallway.

Alma lay back on the soft bed and gazed at the room in all its glory. It had been a long day - a big day - and too many surprises. She felt tired but the recent, new experiences rushed around in her mind. Closing her eyes didn't help either. She turned this way, rolled that way, stretched her legs, re-adjusted the pillow but sleep would not come.

She wondered what the holiday camp would be like. What does a child supervisor do? Would she be able to do Lemmy's work properly? Atty had said she would fill her in on all the details later, and there was no need to be worried as their father owned the camp anyway.

Night was approaching through the curtains. As it was still early, she decided to go for a walk in the gardens.

The back garden extended down a gentle slope that led into a group of trees.

Alma sat down on the grass for some time, hoping the fresh air would clear her head.

Pinpricks of light moved slowly across the darkening sky. Millions of stars filled the heavens above.

The idea of being in America was beyond her wildest dreams, not to mention all the other fantastic things she had seen. Tiredness could definitely be felt, but it wasn't overwhelming her in the usual way.

Still feeling a little jittery she walked down the slope towards the group of trees. The tall trees stood perfectly still in the early night. Their silence drew her closer. A sort of peaceful feeling gave her courage to go further into the forest.

Alma listened to the total silence. How wonderful, she thought.

She could almost hear her own thoughts jumping around inside her mind. Then a muffled noise far off interrupted her peacefulness.

Alma hesitated.

The noise became grunts, then shouts. Other noises became clearer as she walked closer. Was someone in trouble?

Shuffling, groans and loud thuds seemed to come closer to her. She stopped, frightened that she would be discovered.

Someone was running, but not towards her.

As she crept closer, through the trees, the night darkened further.

Suddenly two figures rolled towards her feet, wrestling and shouting.

One of the naked men jumped to his feet and kicked at the other. Soon both were standing and punching vicious blows.

As they moved away from Alma, still fighting, she could vaguely make out their appearances. They seemed to wear nothing but headbands and waist belts - much the same as the rebels, in the caves of Australia.

The only noticeable difference was the long straight black hair.

Alma didn't know whether to run or stay still.

If she tried to move, they might hear her and come after her. But they seemed to be more interested in fighting each other.

The fight moved toward her again.

The two men yelled and grunted as they threw every ounce of energy into the fight.

Before Alma could sense what had happened both men were almost upon her.

She froze.

One of the men stopped halfway through a punch and stared as she half-hid behind a tree.

She wanted to run like mad but couldn't move her legs.

Then, to her surprise, both men took several steps backwards. Slowly they moved away, until they vanished into the dark.

The heartbeats pounded in her chest. Still, she couldn't move!

Noises of the men, fighting again, drifted over to where she stood. They were fighting again! What was happening? Why were they fighting?

Alma took a step backwards. Her legs had moved! It was time to get out of there. She didn't care why the men were fighting.

The trees stood like ghostly figures as Alma dodged them in her mad rush to get away. All she wanted right now was the security of the bedroom in Atty's house.

She ran through the forest. Where was the house?

Surely she hadn't gone that far away. Where was it?

Panic set in. She could feel the grief building up inside.

Something ahead glowed in the dark!

She felt instant relief. It must be the house.

As Alma approached she could see more clearly. It wasn't the house!

She looked all around the forest but there were no signs of a house or anything familiar, except this strange cone like building - glowing in the dark.

She stopped and stared, not knowing which way to go.

Suddenly a dark figure appeared by the side of the tent-like structure.

"Who is it?" called the old man.

Alma could make out his figure against the bright wall of the tent.

Smoke rose from the top of the tent.

It must be an old man camping out in the woods, she thought.

"Who's there?" he called again.

Alma looked around to try to find her bearings - to try to find something that would show her the way to Atty's house. It was no good. All that surrounded her were trees, and more trees, illuminated by the old man's bright tent.

She jumped in fright as someone touched her shoulder.

"Are you lost?" said the old man in a slow croaking voice.

Before she could answer or run away, the old man walked towards his tent. He waved a hand to Alma.

"Come. I will show you the way back to the town."

He disappeared behind the tent.

Alma thought for an instant, before making a move.

He must be a hundred years old! The long white hair could easily be seen in the dark. Surely he couldn't pose a threat - not at his age.

Undecided whether to run or not, she finally moved closer to the tent so as to get a better look. Keeping a safe distance she circled the tent. The old man had gone inside. Alma could see his shadow on the wall as he sat down next to the fire, in the centre of the circle.

He waved his hand again.

"Come in."

Alma bent down and peered in through the tent door. He sat alone.

She raised her head and carefully listened to the forest but could not hear the two fighters anymore.

"I just want to get back to the house. It can't be that far from here."

The old man didn't appear to hear her.

"Come in," he slowly repeated.

His voice sounded so gentle and soft. Alma instantly took to liking him. She peered again through the door at the old figure sitting and staring into the fire.

She tried again.

"I just want to get back to Atty's house."

It was useless. He didn't budge.

Alma gave in and entered the huge tent.

He waved a hand and signalled for her to sit near the fire.

A fur rug warmed her bare legs as the fire glowed with heat. Smoke spiralled up out through a hole in the top of the tent.

Alma looked into the old man's eyes. He must be the oldest person she had ever come across.

His face was covered in weathered lines, yet there was something strange about his eyes. They seem to be so youthful. As she looked, a force seemed to pull her in towards his eyes - black pools of emptiness.

It was as if the black eyes were holes and she was falling into them, with nothing to grab hold of.

She couldn't stop herself.

Alma blinked again and again to try and break the spell but it was no good.

She tried to speak, hoping that might break his spell.

"I'm lost. I just want to go home to Atty's house," she eventually pleaded.

The old man slowly lifted his arm and pointed off to the left. He held his gaze all the while.

It was obvious he wasn't going to say any more, so Alma stood up and prepared to leave. He pointed again to the left.

"Thank you." Alma walked out into the forest, heading in the direction the old man had shown. Within minutes she could see lights through the trees.

She ran flat out till she was safely behind the door of the kitchen in Atty's house.

"Alma! Breakfast!" sang Atty.

Alma opened her eyes and looked around the room. She was in bed!

And she was in Lemmy's bedroom!

She stretched and yawned.

Was that a dream? Had she dreamt about the men fighting? What about the old man?

She tried to retrace her steps the previous night. It seemed so real! As Alma dressed for breakfast she tried to recall the face of the old man.

All of a sudden those strange empty black eyes zoomed in on her mind's eye. She jerked backward and fell onto the bed in fright.

"Deborah Clearwater."

The old man's face spoke to her - in her mind - as she sat on the bed.

He smiled but there was a kind of sadness in his eyes.

"Deborah Clearwater," he repeated.

His face vanished.

Alma searched all around the room. Was this some sort of trick? Is this the way these Americans get a laugh? She hesitated. No! Atty wouldn't pull a trick like that.

Am I going crazy?

What is this?

Who is Deborah Clearwater?

It wasn't a dream! That voice had just spoken to her and it was as real as Atty's voice calling out to her for breakfast. It was as if the old man had been in the room - loud and clear.

She finished dressing and joined Atty at the breakfast table.

Alma decided to keep it to herself for the time being. Maybe she would tell Atty later.

PART TWO

CHAPTER FIVE

Castle Rock looked like any other city Alma had seen in her recent travels.

The sleek black air-car flew over the buildings and on towards the children's camp some miles out of town.

A big red sign greeted Alma and Atty as they stepped out of the air-car.

'CASTLE ROCK HOLIDAY CAMP'

The automatic air-car shot up into the sky and vanished amongst the white clouds.

What a complete contrast to the compound in Australia, thought Alma. They walked along the shiny footpath. Birds and butterflies fluttered among the richly decorated flowerbeds. Fountains of water streamed forth from every different angle.

Children rushed about, screaming and laughing at the top of their lungs.

In the staff office Mrs. Hemp went over the routine of the camp with Alma. Atty had already left.

"Now, Alma," she said. "Are there any questions?"

"No."

"You'll soon get used to the set-up. Just do what the other staff members do. You're only here for two weeks, so take it easy. Have some fun."

Alma smiled at the old lady and followed her over to her new work space.

"There are girls and boys of all ages, from all over the world," shouted Mrs. Hemp.

Alma nodded and looked at the many different styles of clothing the children wore as they raced along the footpaths.

Mrs. Hemp pointed towards long barracks and turned to walk in that direction.

"They come here for ten weeks at a time. The camp stays open all year round."

"Who pays for it?" said Alma.

"Atty and Lemmy's father owns and runs it but the USSF of A Government foots the bill. The camp helps younger generations from other countries to become acquainted with the rapidly advancing technologies of America. People become antagonistic when they can't understand their neighbours. So we help them to understand our new ways."

"Why is it that America can advance way ahead of the rest of the world?" asked Alma.

"A great man lived in America some generations ago. He developed major breakthroughs in many different fields of technology - the most significant being the field of the mind. It's just that we cottoned on to it faster than the rest of the world. You know - him living in America and all that."

"What was his name?"

"Here we are?" said Mrs. Hemp. She walked through the automatic doors and showed Alma into the staff office.

"You'll find out about his name and other things in good time. This is Julie. You'll be working with her for most of your stay. Bye."

"Hi! And this is Dwight," said Julie, pointing to her assistant.

They both smiled and shook hands with Alma.

"Where's Lemmy?" asked Dwight.

"She'll be back in a couple of weeks," said Alma.

"I'll bet Lemmy has a new boyfriend in Australia," laughed Julie.

Alma smiled but didn't answer.

Julie and Dwight were about the same age and probably a little older than herself, thought Alma. Both had blonde hair and very bronze-tanned skin.

"Here's your cap. All the staff wear them," said Julie.

While Alma adjusted the size of the cap, Dwight pinned a badge to her shirt.

"Here's your badge. All the staff wear them," he smiled.

Alma walked behind the counter to join the other two, who had already set off to show her about.

Julie pointed from the counter down along one of the long corridors of shelves.

"This is where the sports equipment goes out and comes back in. We keep everything on those shelves.

You'll get the chance to have a closer look later. It's simple enough - we are definitely not overworked around here. Someone from one of the camp sections comes in, gives us an order form, we give them the sports gear, he or she signs for it and takes the lot away for the day. At the end of the day the gear comes back, we give out a receipt, then we clean the gear and pack it all away till next time."

"Make sure the person asking for the gear has a security badge just like yours," added Dwight.

"Today's Monday. That means cleaning for most of this morning," smiled Julie. "Dwight! She's all yours. Have fun!"

"Come on. I'll show you the ropes," said Dwight.

Alma and Dwight spent the morning cleaning the inside of the building and the gear. As Dwight liked to talk, Alma found out all that she wanted to know about the holiday camp.

It took two thousand children at a time. Besides sport, the children learnt a new method of study and philosophy, a little music and art, and got a brief indoctrination on the newest and latest advances in technology - in almost every field of science.

Dwight ran out of things to talk about and so began whistling quietly as he worked.

Alma, with some hesitation, finally came out with the question she had wanted to ask someone since first thing this morning.

"Dwight? Have you ever heard of a girl by the name of Deborah Clearwater?"

Dwight smiled and his face lit up, showing off his dazzling white teeth.

184

"Who hasn't? Deborah Clearwater is the greatest singer that America has ever known.

"Everyone adores her. Can you believe that? And only sixteen years old! And the longest blonde hair you could ever imagine."

Alma had never seen anyone so impressed by another person as Dwight was of this Deborah Clearwater.

He went on:

"You mean to say that you've never heard of her?"

Alma shook her head.

"I've only heard of her name."

"Wow! Alma. Where have you been for the past two years?"

Alma shrugged her shoulders and attempted a smile.

"How do I go about seeing her?"

"You don't," said Dwight. "She just turns up uninvited at public concerts. No-one ever knows which concert. Some say she is an angel. If you just happen to be at a concert when she miraculously appears, it is like being blessed. It's really mysterious stuff. She doesn't even record any songs on laser either! And people who try to imitate her music - after her shows - never quite get it right. I was lucky to see her once. It was the most rewarding thing I have ever done in my whole life."

"Does she do anything besides sing at concerts?"

"Don't think so," said Dwight. "Oh! I think she has an interest in world peace. You know what I mean?"

They bundled up the hockey sticks that they had just finished cleaning and headed for the shelves.

"You mean that I can't get to meet her?"

"Nope. Sorry."

Alma thought back to the old man in the glowing tent the night before. Was it a dream? How was it that she had been given a real person's name if it was only a dream? And especially when she had never heard of her name before.

Dwight interrupted her thoughts.

"She is supposed to live in a small town down in the south-east, but no-one has ever seen her there. Maybe it's just a rumour. The newspapers and television companies have searched high and low for her, but not a single sign. All very mysterious."

Alma could tell by Dwight's sparkling eyes that he loved the mysterious nature of this girl called Deborah Clearwater.

He went on:

"The newspapers have put up a reward of $200,000 for information as to her whereabouts. Some say she is from another planet and that's why she can cast a spell over all of us. I don't care what they say. I got the chance to see her in person. It was a beautiful experience.

"One last thing," whispered Dwight. "There is a rumour going around that if you travel to a little town way down in the south-east, called Cook Town, you just might be lucky to catch a fleeting glimpse of her. Some people have waited at Cook Town for a month and never seen anything. The rumour says, that to see her, a person must have a very special need.

"Of course there are those who dismiss the whole mystery of Deborah Clearwater as nothing more than a figment of the imagination - a delusion of the nerve impulses, conjured up as a by-product of a chemical imbalance of the brain cells.

"All I can say to that is - I was there man, and I seen her with my own two eyes!"

Dwight began laughing loudly.

The first of many days went by without a hitch.

Before Alma knew it, two weeks had almost flown by so fast that she wondered whether it was real or just a fancy dream.

Three more days and she would be back in Australia.

Walking to the main office to meet Atty after work, she felt a little ashamed because of the doubts that crossed her mind about going home.

Would she enjoy going home? Could she really call Australia home? Somehow it didn't pull at her heart strings as she felt it should. Of course there wasn't a choice. She had to go back. Lemmy would need her passport.

But more importantly, she felt a strong urge to help her own people, even if it was only in the smallest of ways.

Alma smiled as she closed the door behind her in the main office.

Mrs. Hemp smiled back.

"Atty had to supervise the girls' showers. Sarah is off sick. You can wait here if you like - she shouldn't be long."

"It's alright. I'll go over and help."

Alma enjoyed the walk over through the colourful gardens. She would really miss Atty when the holiday finished.

They had become really good friends. Dwight had asked her out , to go see a concert. Atty had laughed at Alma when she had told her the night before. Alma didn't think it right that she should give Dwight any ideas of possible romance and so had refused his offer. Atty had called her a loner. And loners always ended up as spinsters, and lonely, Atty had teased. Alma dismissed the whole thing, there was plenty of time yet for romance. After all, she was only seventeen!

I can't complain, she thought. A trip to America! And meeting people from all over the world. It surely has been a great adventure.

As Alma walked into the shower block, she spotted Atty over in the corner talking to six or seven young dark-skinned girls. Most of them were naked with towels in their hands.

Two of the girls seemed to receive most of the attention and appeared upset. Atty and the others were staring at their bodies.

As Alma approached, one of the two girls murmured:

"We can't help it. This is the way they do things over there."

Alma looked closer. There didn't appear to be anything out of the ordinary.

"I think it's disgusting," said one of the girls in the group.

Two others slowly shook their heads in disbelief.

"How could you let them do it?" said another.

When Alma understood what it was that had the attention of the group, she almost melted on the spot. The shock hit her from head to toe.

She felt utter pity for the two young girls.

"Alright!" said Atty. "The side-show is over. Hurry up! Get dressed and hop it to the mess hall or you'll all miss out on dinner."

Atty shook her head and looked at Alma.

"What happened to them?" whispered Alma.

"It's the custom in certain parts of Africa. It's called circumcision. You've heard how they used to do it to boys last century. Well, in Africa, they still do it to girls."

"But it looked like their private bits have been stitched up! How do they go to the toilet?"

"Shhh!" said Atty. A few of the girls came back over after dressing. "I'll tell you about it on the way home."

Alma sat in silence as the auto-car flew towards Atty's house.

Atty laughed.

"You should see your face! Don't worry about it. I see this sort of thing all the time. That's nothing compared to what some of the other countries send to our camp."

Alma lifted her eyebrows, still shocked at the thought that adults would do such a horrible thing to young girls.

"Those two girls come from a place called Miami, not far from Lake Kariba in Africa," continued Atty. "Millions of girls are circumcised, usually before they reach five or six or seven years of age. It is their custom to sow up the bits, leaving only the size of a pin-hole, just enough room for the usual female functions. Of course, the girls say it becomes very painful if you are ever in a hurry to go to the toilet, and disease is common because they can't get rid of all the blood when the monthly cycle comes around."

Alma looked out the window at the passing clouds.

"Hopefully," continued Atty, "after their short stay with us, these girls won't do it to their kids. Two old African women came over to the camp some years ago. They told me that the custom stretches so far back in time that nobody really knows the proper reason why it is still carried out.

"One of the old women said it stops the adult men from raping the young girls. It also stops the young girls from flirting with married men.

"It also guarantees that men get virgins for brides.

"The other old woman said those reasons might be the driving force behind circumcision today but witchcraft and sorcery have had a strong influence in the past. She said that people still believe in the supernatural.

"The chief man of each village is a white sorcerer who has special magic medicines in his hut to keep away evil black sorcerers. If a woman is menstruating and goes near the chief's magic medicines, it can destroy his power.

"There is supposed to be some confusion as to whether or not the Islamic religion is the cause of this tradition. The old women said there are many Muslims in Africa and menstruating women are forbidden from the mosques and churches.

"One way to keep the chief's power strong, is this circumcision thing.

"She said that there is an even older belief than that one, going back to the beginnings of time itself!

"Girls are supposed to have little evil nature-spirits living inside their vaginas. These little spirits are supposed to fly out in the middle of the night and eat other spirits.

"She said that they can put evil spells on people.

"So that's some of the reasons why the old grandmothers cut out all the flesh and meat - you know, a sacrifice to the spirit of Mother Earth, or to Allah, or who knows what - and then sow them up nice and tight."

Alma shook her head again.

"The grimmest joke is that because the girls can't keep clean, diseases set in and that leads to sterility for many girls."

Alma instantly thought of the story about the poisoned water in the compound at Australwitz One and her own possible sterilization. She quickly dismissed the thought as nothing in comparison to what these poor girls were put through.

"When you see it as often as I do, it's not quite as shocking as it seems. But I can still remember the first time. My reaction was probably the same as yours."

"Why doesn't someone do something about it?" asked Alma.

"It is gradually changing. We don't see as many as the years go by. I've been coming here since I was a kid. Things are slowly changing but there is still a long way to go yet."

"It makes my problems seem so small!" said Alma.

"Don't worry about it, Alma," smiled Atty. "You're on holidays. Look at it as a learning experience. Don't let it spoil your last few days - brighten up! No work! We can go to Denver and let our hair down on your last weekend."

"Atty, I know you had something special planned for this weekend and thanks for everything you've done for me, but I really would like to see if I can find this girl, Deborah Clearwater."

"It's alright. I've got a man in Denver. I'll try to get along without you."

Both girls looked at each other and burst out laughing.

Atty then shook her head and said:

"I don't think you'll find her but go ahead, you'll enjoy the trip. It's nice down in the south-east."

That night Alma snuggled into Lemmy's soft pillow as she tried to go to sleep.

Pictures raced through her mind.

She just couldn't let go of the shocking scene she had seen that day.

How could they do such terrible things to innocent little girls?

Alma tried to think of other things as she lay awake.

Gradually she fell into a half-sleep.

A picture of young girls dancing and singing flashed into her mind. Alma was one of the little girls, holding hands with another.

The sun cast sharp black shadows on the dirt as they raced around in a circle, laughing and singing songs. They were about seven years old.

One girl had a bright red ribbon trailing behind her hair as she spun around. The others clapped and sang. Alma joined in.

She laughed so much that her ribs began to hurt. She held the sides of her stomach but couldn't stop laughing.

"Alma?" called a familiar voice. Her mother waved a hand to her from the door of the grass hut.

She smiled at her mother, so beautiful and tall.

Alma ran over and hugged her mother's skirt. She snuggled into the sweet smelling fabric – her mother smelt so good.

Alma looked up and smiled at her.

"Come on baby. You've got to help me do something special today."

Alma took hold of her mother's hand and followed her.

"Come with me baby," smiled her mother.

"What are we going to do, Mummy?"

Alma always felt so excited when her mother asked her to help out. It made her feel so grown up and special.

"We are going to make some sweet pudding baby," said her mother as they walked towards her grandmother's hut , over past the village centre.

"Sweet pudding!" Alma smiled.

When they reached the entrance to the hut, Alma's mother stepped to the side.

"You go in first baby," she said, pushing Alma in through the door.

Alma's care-free smile quickly turned to confusion as four old women grabbed hold of her.

She fell to the dirt floor. The old women pinned her to the ground by her arms and legs.

"Mummy! Mummy!" cried Alma.

Her mother didn't come.

The old women rolled her over onto her stomach. They pulled Alma's arms behind and tied them together.

When she was rolled over again, onto her back, her mother had disappeared.

Her grandmother smiled down at her.

"Everything will be alright, child," she said with a toothless smile.

"Your special time has come! You are going to be closer to Allah!"

Her grandmother held up a rusty old knife and ran her finger down the blade.

Alma could feel terror flood through her body. What was happening? What was grandmother going to do to her? She began screaming.

"No! No! Get away!"

Two of the old women held her down. Another put her arms on Alma's chest.

Alma kicked and struggled with every fibre in her little body but it was hopeless. Another old woman had her by the legs.

Now two of them held her legs. They held tight around her knees and wrenched them apart.

Alma couldn't move. Four big old women held her down with legs wide apart.

"Mummy! Mummy! I want my Mummy. Stop them Grandma, please! They're hurting me. Mummy! Mummy! Where's my Mummy?"

Her mother never came to help.

She looked up at the roof of the hut and screamed with all her might.

"Please Mummy, don't let them hurt me. Please!"

A sharp pain cut into her.

It was so unbearable Alma almost fainted.

She tried to close her legs to stop the pain.

When she gritted her teeth another piercing stab cut into her.

Immediately, she screamed at the top of her voice.

Someone rammed a piece of wood into her mouth.

"Bite it! Bite it to stop the pain," said an old woman.

"Stop all this crying and screaming," said another. "It doesn't hurt that much. You're just over-acting."

The pain shot through Alma's body, pulling at every nerve until she felt she would soon faint.

Her grandmother continued cutting away at the flesh between Alma's legs.

It was like someone kept stabbing at her with a red hot poker.

Alma tried to kick. She tried to close her legs. She tried to bite the old women.

She growled like a wild animal and screamed at the roof. It was useless. No one would help her.

Why wouldn't her mummy help her?

Blood covered her legs.

As her grandmother continued to cut and scrape away the flesh, Alma began to fade off into a half-sleep.

Moisture trickled down into her eyes. Her whole body was soon covered in sweat and blood.

"Daddy! Daddy! Where's my Daddy? I want my Daddy!"

Alma cried and cried but no-one would listen.

She tried to will herself into unconsciousness but even that wouldn't come.

All a sudden the cutting stopped.

Alma looked up.

To her horror, right before her eyes, a woman passed a long needle and horse-hair thread to her grandmother.

Bloody hands held the needle high, not caring if the girl saw it.

Alma reached a new level of pain as the needle punctured her skin. Her grandmother pulled and yanked at the thread to get it as tight as possible.

The screams increased to a high pitched screech.

"Mummy! Mummy! I want my Mummy!"

"Stop all this nonsense!" scowled her grandmother. "The black sorcerers won't be able to enter your body now. Those evil spirits will fly over you in the middle of the night and search for a victim in some other village. You should think of yourself as a very lucky girl."

Her grandmother looked up at the thatched roof of the hut.

"Yes! You will stay clean. And Allah will protect you."

The stitching stopped.

The old women let go of her legs.

Someone sat her up and untied her hands.

"Now," said her grandmother, "go outside to the village centre. Sing and praise Allah for this wonderful gift."

Two old women lifted Alma to her feet and pushed her out of the hut.

"Dance! Dance! Sing praises to Allah!"

The old women gathered around her. They began stamping their feet and clapping their hands.

"Dance! Sing!"

Blood flowed down Alma's legs, splattering onto the dirt.

The pain was unbearable.

Alma fell to her knees.

She crawled away towards her own hut.

"You are a disgrace to your mother and your family name," said her grandmother, spitting onto the dirt.

The old women grabbed Alma once more. Cloth strips were used to tie her legs together so as to stop the wound from opening.

They carried her towards the family hut.

Alma looked up at the sky.

Dizziness began to overwhelm her.

When she closed her eyes everything went red and she felt as if she was going to be sick.

She quickly opened her eyes again.

Now the thatched roof of her home was above her.

Everything started spinning.

Her mother sat next to her bed, wiping her forehead.

"There, there, now. It's alright. It's all over now."

Alma looked over towards the doorway. Her father quickly glanced away and shamefully bowed his head as he left the hut.

Her mother continued to wipe the moisture from her head.

Alma painfully rolled over to one side, away from her mother.

She didn't want to look at her.

Her parents no longer meant anything to her. They were strangers as far as she was concerned.

She wanted to cry and forgive them. Grown-ups do some stupid things sometimes. She tried to see that they would only do what was right for her, but the reasoning didn't make sense - no matter how she looked at it.

Up till now Alma had always found it within her heart to forgive their sometimes cruel ways, but this time they had gone too far.

Hatred rose up inside her. Blinded by a red rage, she wanted to reach out and scratch out her mother's eyes.

Never! Never! They will never be forgiven for this.

Grief suddenly overwhelmed her.

Alma howled as loud as she could. Tears rushed from her eyes.

She screamed at the top of her voice, and tried to sit up.

Her mother's face suddenly turned into an ugly demon - laughing at her.

Anger shook her.

She reached for the demon's eyes - scratching and clawing like a wild animal.

Suddenly her eyes automatically opened!

She was back in Lemmy's bedroom!

Everything was dark. There were no sounds.

The alarm clock, beside the bed, showed just before midnight.

It had only been half an hour or so since she had first got into bed!

The dream had been so real.

Tears welled up inside her and flowed from her eyes.

Alma buried her head in the soft pillow.

PART TWO

CHAPTER SIX

The sleek black auto-car arrived on time the next morning.

It hovered inches above the ground, waiting for its passenger.

Alma waved goodbye to Atty and slid inside the empty vehicle.

She pushed Lemmy's card into the slot, punched in the security
code and waited.

"Destination?" said a feminine voice, from nowhere in particular.
Alma couldn't locate any speakers in the auto-car.

"Cook Town, please."

"Thank you," said the auto-car. "Destination will be Cook Town,
USSF of America. If you wish to cancel, press the red button now.
Departure will be in ten seconds."

Green numbers counted down from ten on the display screen.

Within seconds the auto-car shot up into the sky and then headed
south-east.

It was a beautiful day.

The sun warmed Alma's arm through the tinted window. White
clouds filled the bright blue heavens.

There was a funny sensation surging through Alma's body. She
hadn't been alone for quite awhile.

It was like a new adventure - even if only for a day or two.

She enjoyed the low flying scenic tour of the south-east of America.

Within no time at all, the auto-car began to slow down.

It then dropped to ground level and hovered inches above the road as it cruised along a giant highway.

When Alma saw the sign - Cook Town - she cringed slightly.

What would she say to this girl if she did happen to run into her?

Maybe it would be a better idea just to forget about it and do some sight-seeing.

No! She decided to go ahead with it. When she returned to Australia, she would be kicking herself, never knowing the full story about Deborah Clearwater, if she stopped now.

Yes! Better not think about it and just do it!

Cook Town was a typical small town.

The auto-car stopped in the centre of the main street - the only street.

Alma got out, looked up and down the sleepy little settlement. Half a dozen houses lined one side of the street, with a general store in the middle.

The other side of the main street was a sandy beach that ran gently down to calm blue water.

Alma walked south along the footpath glancing back and forth from the white houses to the yachts out on the water.

Not a person in sight!

It was very hot. She decided to get a drink from the local store.

"Morning," said the old shop-keeper.

Alma smiled, grabbed a bottle from the fridge and handed some money over the counter.

As the old man gave her the change, he said:

"Passing through or visiting someone?"

"Does Deborah Clearwater live here, in this town?"

"Can't say as I know any-one by that name. And I believe I know everyone in this town."

The old man looked her up and down, then rubbed his chin for some time before continuing:

"You know, a lot of young people - just like you - come down here looking for this so-called person. We keep telling them that no-one by that name lives here but they keep coming, all the same."

"Thank you," said Alma.

She walked out onto the porch and looked at the blue water while she finished her drink.

What a waste of time, she thought.

As Alma approached the auto-car, something that she couldn't quite put her finger on attracted her toward the beach.

She sat down at the water's edge and looked back over her shoulder at the sleepy houses, a hundred yards up the beach. The cool water soothed her feet.

An old woman sat twenty or so yards up the way. She held a fishing line in one hand and smoked a cigarette with the other.

Alma lay back on the warm sand. The sea air smelt good.

With her feet still in the water, she shielded her eyes from the hot midday sun.

It was a different sort of heat to the desert heat of Australia, she thought. Thick moist air made her white summer-dress stick to her body.

The fierce sunrays beat down on her face.

Even with hands shielding her eyes, she could still see the glowing red behind her eyelids.

This is just perfect, thought Alma. What a way to finish off a perfect holiday! She let all her nerves go and relaxed completely.

Soft sounds drifted along the beach.

A cool breeze caressed her cheek.

Her arms fell to the sand and her head rolled to the side as she fell into a half-sleep.

The red turned to white, behind her eyelids.

Suddenly Alma found herself staring at a very big white building. As she walked towards it she could see many windows. It must be over ten stories high.

She stopped to look around.

A beautiful garden surrounded her. She stood in the middle of a white gravel path in the centre.

To get to the building she had to walk under an archway made of huge pine trees curved in toward the centre.

On the left stood a magnificent gold statue of an angel with wings spread wide. The angel smiled down at Alma. A golden book rested in one hand, while the other pointed to delicate gold letters written across the face of the opened pages.

' Future Love Across Galaxies. '

An old man, wearing a sea captain's hat, stepped out from behind the statue. He held a bunch of flowers in one hand and a pair of cutters in the other. He walked down the path without looking at her.

He must be the gardener, thought Alma.

She continued walking toward the big white building.

Steps led her to the massive front doors.

Written above the polished oak doors were the words:

' Lightning Ridge Homestead. '

Before Alma could knock on the door, a big black man magically appeared in the doorway.

He had a big black moustache and what must've been a glass eye. He seemed to be looking in two different directions at the same time.

Alma didn't know what to say. She just stood there.

The big black man smiled and said:

"We've been expecting you, Alma."

Alma felt like a little girl in one of those children's stories they had read at the school back at the compound.

"Follow me."

Alma walked behind him and admired the elegance of the building.

The polished floor of the long hall reflected images like a mirror.

The walls were dark rich wood with carved pictures and the overhead lights made the place sparkle. She passed many doors with numbers written on them.

The only sounds Alma could hear were their footsteps as they headed for the end of the long wide corridor.

Shortly, the big black man stopped at a door at the end of the hall. It had a large gold number - seven - above the entrance.

He knocked quietly before entering.

When inside, he motioned for Alma to take a seat.

The big red leather couch and the cool air gave Alma a sense of easiness but there was still the apprehension of not knowing what was going to happen next.

She tried to straighten out the wrinkles in her old white dress but soon gave it up as a waste of time.

Then she looked around the room. A large picture of a man sitting at the steering-wheel of a boat, wearing a sea captain's cap, caught her attention.

That was the man she had seen in the garden!

He seemed to be smiling down at Alma.

Countless coloured books filled shelves, lining every inch of every wall. Red volumes, green volumes, blue volumes - on and on.

Suddenly, Alma's mouth opened wide when she noticed the names of the authors. It was the same author for every book!

There must be thousands of books! How could one person write so many books?

A cold shiver went down her backbone. This was the same person who had written the old book that she had found in the desert!

How could it be?

He would have written that book one hundred and fifty years ago. Yet, there he was out in the garden - she had seen him!

Glancing around the room, a strange machine, resting on the dark wooden desk, caught her attention.

It looked like some sort of electrical measuring instrument, with two wires attached to the side. The wires were connected to, what looked like, two polished tin soup cans on the desk next to the machine.

The back door opened.

Alma's stomach fluttered and jumped up into her throat.

A beautiful girl, not much younger than Alma and about the same height, walked into the room.

There seemed to be a sphere of bright light surrounding her body.

She smiled and held out her hand as she approached Alma. Long blonde hair hung all the way down past her waist. She was dressed completely in white.

The closer she came, the more Alma could feel some sort of power approaching her - something like an intense concentration of love and peace.

It was like a magnetic force pulling at her and jumping to and fro between them.

This girl is the most beautiful being imaginable, thought Alma. It felt as if it was an honour just to be in the presence of this noble being.

Deborah Clearwater shook Alma's hand and opened her mouth, about to say something.

"Hey! Wake up!"

Someone else now had hold of Alma's hand.

"Are you alright?" said a female voice.

Alma opened her eyes.

"Quick! A storm is coming up fast!" she continued.

The old fishing woman from up along the beach pulled at Alma's arm.

"Come on darling, better hurry. There'll be thunder and lightning soon. Let's get out of here."

In the auto-car, on the way back to Castle Rock and Atty's house, Alma couldn't stop thinking about the dream back on the beach.

Was it a dream? It had to be!

But it felt so real!

Something about it niggled her.

Dream or no dream, she knew that Debbie Clearwater had spoken to her. She knew that they had spoken, but about what she couldn't for the life of her remember. What was it?

PART   TWO

CHAPTER   SEVEN

Alma listened to the pilot speaking over the intercom as she sat in a very comfortable black leather chair.

The disk-shaped aircraft would be taking off for Australia in the next few minutes.

Even the tinted windows couldn't hold out the bright sunshine.

She looked up through the honeycombed ceiling of the aircraft at the blue sky.

Then her eyes focused on the shape of the windows themselves, with their honeycomb pattern.

One, two, three, four, five, six sides.

One, two, three, four, five, six sides.

One, two, three, four, five, six sides.

She smiled to herself when she recalled Atty's farewell hugs and kisses. They were truly friends for life, thought Alma. She wished with all her might that they would see each other again.

Alma's thoughts drifted back to Castle Rock, then Atty's house and then to Cook Town where Deborah Clearwater supposedly lived.

She still couldn't make heads or tails out of it.

Just strange dreams, she told herself.

Yes! Just strange dreams, that's all it is.

The airship lifted quickly and smoothly, high up into the sky.

Straight up!

Passengers in front and beside Alma began to open their individual visual-screens.

Something important must be coming on, thought Alma. Everywhere she looked, people were doing the same. Some were looking at their watches as well.

She followed their cue and pressed the button on the side arm of her chair.

A thin plastic arm shot out, unfolded and extended around to the front of the chair. Then a small white screen unfolded from the end of it, about three feet in front of Alma's face.

Just as she fitted the cordless ear plug speakers, an announcement buzzed into her ear and a picture flashed onto the screen.

"And now, ladies and gentlemen, I have the greatest pleasure in giving you the President of the USSF of America.

"Live, from coast to coast - New York to L.A.

"Broadcast from Alaska and Canada in the north, through all the central states of North America, to all the southern states in South America, from Mexico to Argentina. The great USSF of America! God bless the Americas!

"Yes folks! It's time for the monthly presidential speech!

"Once again, it gives me the greatest pleasure in introducing the President of the USSF of America – Mister Clint Clinton."

A very old man, with white hair, appeared on the screen.

The passengers in the aircraft clapped and cheered.

The president must be at least two hundred years old, by the look him. He moved his hands very slowly and when he laughed, wrinkles lined his face.

Just from the smile alone, Alma felt an affinity for the man.

"Good morning, fellow American citizens!" said the President. "Here we are once again.

"We are now entering the third phase of the master plan.

"Yes! The top-secret, third phase that you have all have been waiting for.

"Phase One has been successful for the past one hundred years – that is, the budget running at a profit.

"Phase Two has also been successful for the past fifty years – that is, no taxes whatsoever.

"And now the time has come to put phase three into action.

"As you all know, I've been the President of the USSF of America for over one hundred years and my time is nearly up.

"I'm getting old! It's time to put the feet up.

"Nothing has meant more to me than the welfare, safety and happiness of the American people. But still, sometimes I wondered why you kept electing me over these many, many years. I thank you from the bottom of my heart for your loyalty.

"There is one thing that has weighed very heavily on my mind. But 'Phase Three' will soon sort that out. I'm only sorry that I couldn't have put it into operation much earlier."

The President looked at his watch and continued:

"In a few minutes, at eleven o'clock, Phase Three will go into effect.

"So! What is Phase Three?

"Phase Three will wipe out the biggest fraud that has been going on for over two hundred years. Yes! We have been lied to, swindled, cheated and ripped off by a - so called - distinguished and professional group of experts for the last two hundred years.

"For now, it doesn't matter how they got away with it for so long. What does matter, is that they have been found out!

"Who are they?

"Well! Let's change the subject for a moment and then get back to the 'who' shortly.

"A very, very old book – a sacred book – states that if the world will be destroyed in the future, it will be done by a great beast-man. And people will know this beast by its number – six, six, six.

"Many prophets and fortune tellers have had visions and gazed into crystal balls to try to foretell the coming of the beast and who it would be.

"These wise men have named many, many evil persons throughout history as 'The Beast'. But, soon after, another beast rears its ugly head and so we have always ended in doubt as to who the real 'Beast' might be.

"A man or beast of the number – six, six, six!

"Excuse me for getting off the track, but all will be revealed shortly – please stay with me.

"We all know that the universe consists of tiny little atoms. From galaxies to planets, from oceans to small puddles, we have atoms, atoms and more atoms.

"Scientists can tell you that the atom is made up of protons and neutrons in the centre, and in orbit around the outside are the electrons.

"Others will tell you that these atoms can be sub-divided further into energy and waves of force.

"The atom is the basic building block.

"Tens of thousands of years ago, wise old men also knew this about the atom. Only recently, old crumpled up manuscripts have been un-earthed from ancient cave-libraries that prove that they did know.

"They also knew, like our modern scientists, that the basic building block of man, and life, is the carbon atom – six protons, six neutrons and six electrons.

"Yes! That's right! Six, six, six!

"The old sacred book of thousands of years ago just might have been more than the ranting and raving of weird tales, as some experts today would have you believe. It might have been right on the mark!

"It talked of a great pretender of knowledge. A destroyer of mankind! It also mentioned that the only thing that would save mankind from this fraud, would be true knowledge."

The President looked at his watch and continued talking.

"What does the carbon atom, the old sacred revelation and the beast have to do with all this?

"Modern leading experts of the mind – the psychiatrists – up till now have had the authority to dictate to the governments around the world what to teach us in our schools, especially about the subject of the mind.

"The only 'mind' the psychiatrist wants to know about is the brain. And the brain, nothing more than flesh, like other organs, is made up of carbon atoms. As far as the psychiatrist is concerned, the only method of thinking available to man is the chemical reactions and the flow of electrical energy between the cells in the brain.

"The main thing wrong with this limited 'brain' theory is that documented evidence proves otherwise. A theory has to be right one hundred percent of the time in all tests and experiments. There can be no exceptions to the rule, otherwise the theory will continually be shown to be false.

"Time and time again, severe head injuries causing mutilation of large sections of the brain have in no way interrupted the ability to think correctly for some patients. Documented evidence exists to prove this.

"Of course, there are many examples proving that brain injuries do disturb the ability to perceive through the senses, but what about the other side of the coin? What about the examples that prove that man can still operate normally with a large section of his brain missing?

"The psychiatrists' brain theory – taught in all schools – fails the basic test!

"So, what does a person really think with? What is the mind? Where does the brain come in within this jigsaw puzzle?

"Well, there has been research going on for many, many years now. This research has come up with a theory that works one hundred percent of the time and I'll be glad to tell you all about that as soon as Phase Three is complete. Those questions will be answered in Phase Four.

"All you need to know for now is that Phase Four will concern the mind and not the brain.

"To think with the brain denies a person of nearly all his mental creativity. A famous scientist tried to tell us this fact, nearly two hundred years ago. And others, later, tried to tell us again, but only a few listened. The brain operates on a reactionary level, a very low level of thinking, if you could call it thinking at all. You know – eat, sleep, sex, eat, sleep, sex … This is the level that any animal operates on. I'm not here today to give anyone a lecture. There are plenty of others more qualified to do that. But to help you understand why we have taken last minute drastic action and implemented Phase Three, I thought I better give you some background data.

"Why would anyone, by implementing false education, want whole populations operating at this animal level?

"And why would anyone preach that the only cure for mental illness would be things that actually destroy mental ability? You know – things like electric shock machines and mind-bending drugs.

"Please excuse my little lecture, but we have been investigating this for some time now and finally the truth can be revealed today.

"For the crimes against humanity, for the irreversible damage to innocent victims and for the destruction of whole cultures, this is what the psychiatric profession deserve and this is what they will get – every last one of them. Fellow Americans - I give you Phase Three."

The screen changed to an image of an army truck.

Two soldiers pointed weapons at three men wearing white coats.

They were being led from a psychiatric hospital and loaded into the back of the army truck.

Then the screen changed to another hospital. The same procedure occurred.

Again! At another psychiatric institution, more were being roughly thrown into army trucks.

The passengers sitting beside Alma clapped and cheered as they watched repeated arrests.

Alma heard someone say:

"Wow! I can't wait to see Phase Four."

PART THREE

CHAPTER ONE

The red sun had already begun its journey down over the horizon when Nurse Shelley started her night shift in the psychiatric wing of the hospital at Australwitz One.

She folded the bed cover back and placed a spare sheet at the end of Jimmy's bed.

Straggly, long, black, curly hair hung down over his eyes.

Nurse Shelley stared at him for a moment, then gazed at the dim light coming through the window.

"What am I going to do with you, Jimmy?" she eventually said.

Jimmy sat up in bed, leaning back against the pillows.

"Come on Jimmy! It's time to go to sleep!"

Jimmy didn't move.

Nurse Shelley shook her head and walked up to the top end of the bed. She tried to push him back down onto the bed but he wouldn't budge.

The same old routine, thought Nurse Shelley. If I don't get you to sleep now, there will be trouble all through the night.

"Lie down!" she yelled.

Jimmy just sat there like a wooden block.

Nurse Shelley could feel the blood pressure rising to the top of her head. She gritted her teeth and pushed harder.

It was useless!

Raising her hand high, she brought it down with all her might and slapped Jimmy hard across the face.

He just continued to stare down at the bed sheet before him.

She slapped him harder! He showed no sign of obedience.

"Auxiliary! Auxiliary!" she shouted down the hall.

Shortly, a big, wide male nursing attendant brushed the curtain to the side as he approached the bed.

"I've already given an injection to sedate him, but it isn't working. I'll have to get Doctor Curr to sort this out tomorrow. The medication just doesn't work on this patient."

The big male nurse grabbed Jimmy around the neck with both hands and shook him. Jimmy remained like a stone.

"Come on, Jimbo!" laughed the male nurse. "Be a good boy."

Nurse Shelley pulled on his feet while the male nurse rough-handled him down flat on the bed.

"There you go! Good lad! That wasn't hard, was it?" chuckled the male nurse.

Jimmy let out a gasp as he attempted to breathe through his damaged windpipe.

Nurse Shelley stepped closer.

"If you do as you're told, this rough treatment wouldn't be necessary. I don't even know why I worry, he'll be getting zapped soon. That'll soon take the stiffness out of him."

Jimmy lay on the bed and stared at the ceiling. His breathing was heavy and difficult.

Nurse Shelley and the attendant laughed as they pushed their way through the curtain.

A faint noise that sounded like a ruffled bed sheet stopped Nurse Shelley in her tracks. She quickly turned and flung the curtain back to peer in at Jimmy.

There was no sign of him trying to move. He lay as stiff as a board.

As she walked off down the corridor, something kept niggling at her mind.

She could have sworn that she saw Jimmy's eyes glaring at her, through all that straggly hair.

No, she told herself. It's just the recent late nights catching up on me. Well, that's all right, she smiled. Holidays start soon - two glorious weeks!

Ten minutes later, Nurse Shelley looked at her watch.

"That's the lot. Time for a cuppa," she said to herself.

As she walked through the reception area, on her way to the kitchen, the night attendant smiled and said:

"I've got to go down to the medical wing for about an hour. They need a hand. Can you manage till I get back?"

"Yes. Everything is in order. I'm just having a break. I'll be a good little girl and watch the phone for you. Go ahead."

With a hot cup of tea in her hand, she kicked off her shoes and relaxed in a chair.

The steam wafted up under her nose and smelt good. She slowly swivelled in the chair.

Something caught her attention out of the corner of her eye.

A black shadow or something dark flashed past the reception door. Nurse Shelley listened for sounds. There were no footsteps.

Silence!

She let out a sigh of annoyance as she slipped her tired feet back into her shoes.

As she passed through the doorway into the corridor, a big black form suddenly appeared in front of her.

She let out a gasp and instinctively jumped back in fright.

It was too late.

A big black pair of hands closed tight around her throat.

Before she could scream, one of the hands smothered her mouth.

Down she went, slowly, until she lay flat out on the floor.

Evil eyes glared at her through straggly black hair. Jimmy sat on top and moved his hands so that they covered her mouth and nose.

Nurse Shelley struggled. She tried to bite him. She threw her head to the side. Her fingernails clawed at his arms.

It was no good.

His face began to fade. Then the lights darkened to a bright red before going completely black.

Almost as sudden, the light of the room flashed on again. It was as if she had lost consciousness for a few seconds, then just as quickly regained it.

Nurse Shelley couldn't believe what she was seeing!

How could this be happening?

High up, in one of the corners of the ceiling, she looked down at her body lying on the floor. The weird thing was that she knew her body still had life in it! She could still feel its sensations.

Jimmy, black and naked, had dragged her body further into the reception area. Now he straddled her, pushing her white nursing uniform up and over her knees and still further up to her waist.

Shock and surprise hit Nurse Shelley all at once.

Shock at the realisation of being a spirit, outside her body. And surprise at watching this naked black madman, not knowing what he would eventually do.

Then Jimmy pulled her underpants down to her ankles.

Just when Nurse Shelley had made up her mind as to what was going to happen next, Jimmy stood up and looked around the room. Searching along the kitchen bench-top and pulling drawers open, he couldn't find what he was looking for.

His attention went to the front desk.

Slowly he walked over to the front desk, as if he had all the time in the world.

When he couldn't find what he was after, the search returned to the drawers. In the third drawer, he stopped, and pulled out a small hypodermic needle, wrapped in plastic.

Nurse Shelley hovered above her body as it lay on the floor. Somehow she felt unconnected to the body, but at the same time, some type of beam of energy wouldn't let her leave it, except to keep a safe distance.

Look at it, she thought. The whites of the eyes stared up at her, as if it could see her, as if pleading for her to do something. But was it dead or alive?

Jimmy grabbed a flower vase from the bench, took out the flowers and poured some of the water over his right hand. Then he carefully placed the hypodermic needle in his hand, so as to point it up towards the tips of his fingers.

The needle plunger rested in his palm while his fingers and thumb held the needle. The needle extended just beyond his fingertips.

Nurse Shelley looked on in horror when Jimmy parted her legs with his knee.

Slowly he began to slip his hand up between her legs – the hand that held the needle.

Her body moved slightly, and the chest rose and fell in a sigh.

Could the body be aware of what's happening? No, it's not possible. It must be unconscious.

When the body inhaled, Jimmy pushed up inside it a little. And then, when the body exhaled, he would stop pushing.

Again and again, on every inhale, he gradually worked his arm up inside her body.

She could see his arm slowly disappearing up inside the body. He must be up into its womb!

Still further up he went – up under the ribs.

Nurse Shelley, being separated from the body, couldn't pick up any emotions or pain now, but a thought suddenly occurred to her. My heart!

He's after my heart!

Leave it alone!

It was too late.

Jimmy stopped briefly and then gave a short, sharp jerk of his arm.

Slowly he pulled his arm out.

The syringe was now full of blood! Dark, rich, red blood!

Jimmy held the needle up as he moved around to the head of the body. Carefully he lifted up the head, then the shoulders, until the body sat upright.

Blood began to flow out between the legs. He looked around the reception area, grabbed a box of tissue papers from the bench and put the whole lot in between the legs.

The body now sat up on its own – without any assistance needed. But it still seemed to be unconscious.

Within seconds he pulled the wad of blood-soaked tissues away and threw them in the bin.

The blood flow had stopped.

Next, Jimmy reached for a clipboard from the front desk. After removing the paperwork, he squirted the syringe all over the clipboard. Blood covered all of one side of it.

Then he took hold of the pen that was tied to the clipboard and let the whole thing dangle over the head of the body as it sat on the floor. With its head slightly leaning forward, it looked like a willing sacrifice.

Slowly he began to whirl the clipboard in a circle, just above the head of the body.

Jimmy gradually spun it faster and faster, and the head of Nurse Shelley's body began to sway slightly.

The clipboard hummed as it whirled.

The faster it went, the more the body responded. Now its legs stretched out and its head straightened.

Nurse Shelley hovered above helplessly.

She gasped in horror when a gas-like form drifted up from her body. It looked like an ancient, decayed spirit! Had it been occupying her body? Without her knowledge?

Slowly it floated over towards Jimmy's chest and entered his body, just about where his heart would've been.

He let out a gasp of air, took a deep breath and closed his eyes briefly.

It was as if he experienced some sort of satisfaction from the transfer.

Then he looked back down at the body. It began to breathe heavier as he continued to whirl the clipboard.

Jimmy then put the clipboard down on the bench and stood over the body with his feet either side of its legs. He worked up and down the body, straightening its fingers and toes, over and over again.

The body of Nurse Shelley started to breathe more heavily, suddenly gasped and then threw its head back. With eyes blinking, it seemed to regain consciousness and looked up at Jimmy.

He slid the underpants back up over its thighs, pulled the nursing uniform back down over the legs and stood back.

"Stand up!" said Jimmy.

The body stood up.

"Walk over there and sit down," ordered Jimmy.

The body did as he said.

Nurse Shelley, still stuck up in the corner of the ceiling, thought that Jimmy seemed to be in a trance. But it was like he had done this sort of thing many times before.

He spoke very mechanically - like a zombie or a machine.

As if controlled by something or someone, his actions were more like those of a robot.

Nurse Shelley watched in amazement as her body stood up, walked over and sat down at the bench. It looked straight ahead at the white wall, picked up the cup of tea and acted as if nothing had happened.

Jimmy walked over to it and whispered:

"You will live for only three days. The first day you will be happy and cheerful and laugh. Then, on the next day, you will get a sick stomach."

The body sipped at its cup of tea and continued to stare at the wall.

"On the third day you will die," said Jimmy.

After burying the needle under rubbish in the bin, he wiped the blood off the clipboard and hid the dirty tissues at the bottom of the waste bin.

Scattering the remaining tissues on top of the rest of the waste in the bin seemed to satisfy him. He quickly looked around the room as he walked out.

Nurse Shelley couldn't believe it!

The body down below, sitting there drinking tea, seemed so alien. It was not her body anymore! It was like an egg, with just the shell remaining and all the substance gone. The life-giving contents had been sucked out.

She couldn't do anything about it.

She had no control over it.

Shortly, the night attendant walked into the reception.

"Everything alright?" he said.

"Fine. How was it over there?" said the body, turning to look at the attendant.

"Alright now. You going for your meal now?"

"Yes."

The body stood up and walked out of the room.

What happens now? She panicked. I'm stuck up here.

Suddenly a force pulled at her - something like a magnet.

She began to move through the wall and instantly found herself hovering outside, above the compound hospital, in the twilight of the night.

Then the force pulled her towards the camps of the aborigines out in the compound.

Campfires burned bright in the coming of the night.

She glanced down at a figure running from a campfire toward a tin hut.

For some unknown reason she floated down and followed the vague black figure into the hut. Candlelight lit up a small room.

The figure was a young woman. She now lay on a blanket on the dirt floor, holding her oversized belly.

The young woman, no more than seventeen or eighteen, threw back her head, gritted her teeth in pain and gave out a low moan.

She raised herself up on her elbows and spread her legs wider.

Before Nurse Shelley could try to understand what was about to happen to her, the invisible force sucked her down into the woman's belly.

Moments later a new born baby attempted to cry and was instantly shoved onto the nipple of a warm breast.

"There! There! Beautiful little baby! It's alright," whispered the new mother.

PART THREE

CHAPTER TWO

Jimmy sat up in his bed when he heard all the yelling going on outside in the hospital corridor.

A man shouted.

"You lot are going to pay for this."

"Please Mister Thompson, just take this medicine and leave the hospital. You are being signed out! Please leave," said the day nurse.

Even though Jimmy couldn't see past the closed curtains, he recognised Mop Thompson's voice.

"You'll pay for this, white trash!" Mop shouted at the top of his voice.

"Please Mister Thompson, you must leave," pleaded the nurse.

"Tell that midget doctor to get out here. I'll ring his neck for what he's done to me."

The male nursing attendant was the next to speak.

"We can do this the easy way or the hard way."

"Go to hell, whitey. Get that midget in the white coat, I want to see him. Never mind. I'll find him myself."

Jimmy heard a loud crash. A heap of coloured tablets came rolling in under the curtain. White, red and blue pills lay scattered all over the floor next to his bed.

"Right! That's it! Come on, you're going back out to the compound. And you're going out right this minute," grunted the male attendant.

Jimmy could hear a lot of shoving and sliding and yelling coming from the corridor.

At the speed of a magician his hand dived toward the floor and scooped up two half-full medicine bottles. He emptied each of the white plastic bottles under his pillow, then quietly put them back down on the floor.

The scuffle outside the curtain continued, gradually moving down the hall towards the exit.

A door slammed and everything went quiet.

The nurse pulled the curtain back.

"Dear, oh dear! Look at this mess."

Jimmy watched the nurse clean up the spilt psychiatric drugs. He also watched the little red devil dancing on her head as she crawled around the floor picking up the tablets one by one.

When she was satisfied that she had retrieved all the tablets, the nurse smiled at Jimmy and left, pulling the curtain drawn.

The little red devil jumped from the nurse's head to stand at the foot of Jimmy's bed. It laughed and giggled and jumped about.

"Go on Jimmy! Swallow all of them. You'll feel really good. That quack hasn't been giving you a high enough dose. Go on! They'll make you feel so good you will be able to get in touch with your kin in the Dreamtime."

Jimmy pulled the coloured pills out and held them in his hand. He gave it little thought, especially as the devil had never been wrong before.

The little angel that used to argue with the devil had disappeared long ago. That proved the devil was right. It was the devil that had told him to do those things to that night nurse. And look! She was gone!

Why the hell not!

He threw the twenty or thirty pills into his mouth and grabbed a glass of water from the side cabinet to wash them down his throat.

Within a few minutes the devil disappeared.

Jimmy's body began to tremble after about half an hour. His heart beat faster and faster. A strong, buzzing feeling shot up his spine and tingled the top of his skull.

The devil re-appeared as a thin red gas and exploded in every direction, followed by a weird evil laugh that echoed in Jimmy's ears.

Jimmy laughed.

Hey! This isn't so bad. It's the first time I've felt like laughing in months.

Then, to add to his delight, the room went brighter than bright, even though it was after six in the evening and the lights weren't yet turned on.

But then his lips went numb, and his breathing became irregular.

Jimmy gasped for air but his lungs felt full of water.

His stomach started churning.

Oh no! Pressure built up behind his eyes until the eyeballs felt like they were going to pop out of his head any second.

His vision turned completely red. All he could see now was the colour red.

Jimmy could feel something move through his body. He tried to hold the cheeks of his bottom together as he anticipated what was about to happen. It was no use. A loud rumble, followed by a big spurt, erupted under his bottom.

He squirmed in his hospital bed as a terrible smell wafted up to his nose.

The red behind his eyes changed into blackness.

Then all of a sudden the lungs closed up tight. Jimmy heaved his chest and opened his mouth wide in a desperate attempt to get air. It wouldn't come.

As he lay in bed, his head felt like it was going to explode.

Air! Air! Give me air! The thoughts were as solid and as loud as spoken words but they never went further than his mind.

Jimmy's heart stopped beating and everything went dead quiet. All sensation stopped.

I must be unconscious! It's all black and I can't feel anything, but I can still think - I'm still here!

Suddenly, a voice came drifting in toward him. It was very faint at first but gradually turned from a whisper to a shout.

"Jimmy! Wake up! It's time for your medicine."

He could recognise the nurse's voice. The sound came to him as if through a thick veil. He knew he wasn't hearing it with his ears but more like hearing it as if someone spoke to him in a dream.

It was a sort of a knowingness, instead of the senses, that allowed him to be aware of what was happening.

Then he suddenly realised that the nurse must be shaking his body. This was when he came to understand that he was located in his skull. This was when he suddenly realised that his body had died and that he was a spirit trapped inside his skull.

The problem now was that he could feel his awareness shrinking. Going from being about the size of his skull, he was gradually being sucked inwards and finally reduced to a minute black pea within a single cell.

It must be those damn pills, he thought.

"What's the problem?" said another female voice.

"I think he's dead. There's no pulse. Get the doctor, please nurse," said the first nurse.

Then the male nursing attendant added some words. He must've walked in shortly after the two nurses.

"Excuse me nurse, but I think I know what happened. I counted the pills while separating them, after you cleaned up the spillage, and it appears that half the drugs are missing. Jimmy must've taken them. He must've swallowed them."

A pause! Complete silence! Then:

"He's dead," said a nurse. "Go and get Doctor Curr. If he isn't back yet, get the medical doctor from the medical wing."

Shortly, he had the vague feeling of the hospital bed being wheeled down the corridor.

A heavy black fog stretching out into eternity surrounded Jimmy's limited consciousness. How can I fight something like this, he thought. The anxiety built up gradually.

Then the bed came to a halt. His white hospital gown was removed and his body lifted onto a concrete slab. Next came silence - on and on and on it went.

It must be night time! I must be in the morgue! Where's the doctor? No! He can't help me! Doctors don't believe in spirits.

Help! Help! Someone please help me!

Let me out! Please, please, someone get me out of here.

The silence went on for what seemed like eternity.

Finally a voice filtered through. Was it a dream?

"No need for an autopsy, nurse," said a male voice. "We'll just put heart failure down on the death certificate. We don't want any unnecessary paper work, do we?"

"Yes sir," replied a nurse.

Jimmy recognised Doctor Curr's voice. He tried to call out, in the hope of reaching someone.

"Help! I'm in here! Do something to get me out of here!"

"Get the two black employees, Loo and Fish, to locate the relatives of the deceased. There's no point in keeping the body here. They might as well bury it as soon as possible. Anyway, we need the space in here."

"Yes sir," said the nurse.

Jimmy heard the door shut and then the dreaded silence haunted him once more. He looked around at the eternal blackness and decided that it was more terrifying than the silence. A deep dark apathy, like none before, overwhelmed him. He wanted to cry but couldn't.

The silence slowly dragged on.

A loud clicking noise pulled him from an uncomfortable dream.

The door! Someone was there, at the door!

Jimmy could hear voices. He recognised some of his family. He heard Loo speaking as well.

"Well, let's take him out now."

"Aren't you going to get the doctor's signature of release first, Loo?"

"No, no. It's alright. He said we could take him."

"Poor old Jimmy - he wasn't that old you know."

"This damn hospital! Too many people come out of here, feet first!"

"What was wrong with him anyway?"

"Don't know."

"Me neither."

"I think it was headaches or a stiff neck, or something like that."

"Well, you won't hear me complaining of any aches or pains if this is where you end up."

"Come on! Too much jibber jabber. Let's get out of here. I got other jobs to do besides standing around here all day chin-wagging."

"Yeah! Let's get going - this place gives me the creeps. It's full of evil."

Jimmy listened, trying to work out who the different voices belonged to. He knew it was useless to try to talk to them but he gave it one last shot.

"Help! Help! I'm stuck inside this head! Someone cut my head open. Someone please do something!"

Nothing!

No one listened. No one could hear him.

"Come on Jimmy, let's get you out of here. Let's get you buried and at peace with yourself, so you can go back to the Dreamtime, back to your Waterhole."

"Don't tell me you still believe in that mumbo jumbo?"

"Well, not really - but I think poor old Jimmy did."

"Oh yeah! That's right! His grandfather used to fill his head full of all those old stories."

Jimmy became aware of movement. He heard the truck start up and take off. People shouted above the roar of the engine. The truck stopped a few times and then continued on its way for awhile.

More voices talked and shouted over the noise of the truck.

Finally the truck stopped and digging began.

Shovels were rammed into the desert sand and slowly the dirt piled up next to the body.

"I still think we should bury him the old way."

"Oh! Shut up, old woman."

"Yeah! Those days are long gone, Mary."

"His ancestors would like it done that way."

"Nobody cares about that mumbo jumbo these days."

"What's the old way, Gran?"

"You're supposed to burn the body, and then smash the bones and the skull before you bury them. I don't know why you do it that way, but the old people used to say if you didn't, bad luck would surely follow."

"Listen to this old witch! What a load of crap!"

"Come on boys, let's put him in quick before this old girl has us reading the bible over him as well."

"Yeah! Come on!"

Jimmy suddenly realised they were moving his body and dreaded what would happen next. He wished with all his heart that the old grandmother had been allowed to have her way. Burning and bone-smashing would've been more than welcome right now.

The shovels started up again. Dirt flew about the body. Slowly the sounds of the people disappeared. Then the dreaded silence followed.

Jimmy tried with all his might – what little was left – to get out of his skull but to no avail. It was useless!

No! No! No!

Some one, please help me! Please! Please don't leave me here!

Almost instantly, with the silence and the loneliness - the real torture had begun.

Jimmy screamed and screamed and screamed...

PART THREE

CHAPTER   THREE

Alma glanced over the three-dimensional, glossy pages of the latest air-ship magazine.

The pilot, over the loud speaker, had just told the passengers that they would soon be landing in Australia. She could hardly wait! Only a couple of weeks had passed, and even though the trip to the USSF of America had been beyond her wildest dreams, she now knew what it was to be madly homesick.

She flipped another page, to show the centre pages of the magazine. Different coloured lines criss-crossed over a picture of the world, outlining the major routes this particular airship company travelled when flying around the planet.

She also noticed that the major continents were shown in different colours and on looking closer, it was plain to see that all countries on each continent had united to form allegiances.

She began to realise that the education in the compound was way out of date.

Scotland, Ireland and Australia were among the few that didn't belong to such unions.

England and Wales had joined The United States of the Supreme Fatherland of Germany, which spread from Portugal in the West to the eastern tip of Russia.

Japan and all the south-eastern countries had joined The United States of the Sichuan Flag of China. India had joined the Arab countries and was now part of The United States of the Sura Fundamentals of Islam. The United States of the Spiritual Forces of Africa included Egypt. And the USSF of America owned most of what was left over, across the planet.

This wasn't anything like what her people were being taught at the school in the compound. Alma could only feel disgust towards the Australian authorities for not even bothering to update the school textbooks.

The books at the compound must be leftovers from at least one hundred years ago, she thought.

Alma put the magazine down and began her mental preparation for the dreaded walk through immigration. It had been a harrowing experience on the way out of Australia, but at least Atty had been there to sort things out.

This time she would be on her own.

She double and triple checked her appearance. Lemmy's tight blue jeans; her multi-coloured, flesh revealing top; her wacky shoes with miniature silver 'Liberty Statues' sticking up from the toes; and the sleek black sunglasses - yes, it seems to pass as 'All American'.

Her long, straight black hair was the only thing that Alma hadn't changed. The nervousness coursed through her body. To match the passport photo, her hair should be frizzy. The last time, Atty and Lemmy had put hundreds of thin plaits through her hair but this time there would be none.

Admittedly, the immigration official hadn't even bothered to look up when she passed through, on the way out of Australia. Hopefully, thought Alma, she would get another official as easy going as the last.

The airship shot straight down to earth as if someone had dropped it from a dizzy height high up in outer space.

Not even the smallest of jerks, thumps or vibrations could be felt when it touched down at the Sydney Air Terminal.

Alma forced her body to get out of the seat and follow the crowd of passengers.

The butterflies fluttered throughout her whole body.

The immigration official stared at her as she waited for Lemmy's passport to be returned.

Usually, they just let them run through on the conveyor belt system. Why was she singling me out, thought Alma, as the beads of sweat oozed out of her forehead.

Suddenly the whole air terminal closed in on her. All the hundreds of travellers queuing or rushing or staring off into space seemed to overwhelm her. The only thing on her mind now, was where to run. Then the horrible thought crashed home. There was no-where to run.

What if she was thrown out of her own country! What if they found something wrong with the passport and she could never return to her homeland! No!

Security guards were everywhere! With their necks straining above the general crowds, they looked like turkeys trying to spot the whereabouts of the cunning fox.

"This queue is for Australian citizens only. Could you please take this over to the other queue - the visitor's queue," said the official. She pointed to the ten or so queues on the other side of the railing. "You are visiting, aren't you?" The official looked Alma up and down, smiled briefly, and handed over the passport.

Alma returned the smile, nodded and walked over to join the visitor's queue.

Her body, feeling as light as a balloon and if just released to float high in the sky, coasted in slow motion as she walked out to the reception area where Lemmy stood waving her arms.

I'm home! Alma glanced back at the exit from the immigration room.

Never again!

"Alma!" squealed Lemmy.

Nathan, Lemmy's boyfriend, stood by with thumbs in pockets while the girls hugged. After a couple of weeks in America, Alma was slowly coming around to the idea of Whites and Blacks together, in relationships, but it still left her slightly cold.

"We've got a welcoming-home surprise for you. Come on, I'll tell you about it on the way," giggled Lemmy.

"Atty made me swear that I'd see to it that you were on the next plane to America," smiled Alma.

"She's my sister, not my mother. Don't worry girl, I swear that I'll get the next airship out of here as soon as we finish with your welcoming-home surprise. Is that a deal?"

Alma couldn't do anything about it and she knew that Lemmy knew it as well. She just shook her head and smiled.

"I won't be needing these anymore," said Alma, passing the passport and ID card to her friend. When Lemmy took the passport and handed the ID card back, Alma gave her a questioning look.

"You might need this as security until your travels take you back home," smiled Lemmy. "Come on! Let's go!"

Nathan took Alma's bag and led the way out.

"Yeah! We better get going if we hope to make it there on time," he said.

They were met by another boy sitting in the van. Soon the purple van pulled out of the car park. Alma and Lemmy sat in the back. Alma began answering Lemmy's questions but within minutes the van stopped and they all jumped out.

"Come on Alma, you can tell me the rest on the train," laughed Lemmy.

The train trip was another new experience for her. She sat facing Lemmy and Nathan, who were unashamedly cuddling and kissing on the opposite seat. Nathan's friend sat next to Alma.

"Don't worry about it. You'll soon get used to this." Nathan's friend pointed to the two love-birds across the table. "They do this all the time!"

Alma smiled and then looked out the window, sipping at a milkshake, watching the countryside roll on by.

Gradually, the grass and trees changed from lush green to a lifeless brown.

What could the surprise be? Where are they taking me? We've been on this train for a long time now. The thoughts raced through her mind. When Lemmy refused again and again to tell her, Alma gave in and closed her eyes to let the train noises send her to sleep.

"Here we go! Come on sleepy head!" Lemmy was up and straightening out her skirt in the aisle when Alma opened her eyes.

Canberra! I'd forgotten that this place even existed, thought Alma. That's right! It's the Australian Capital Territory. She remembered being taught about this place in school at the compound.

Walking around the city circle, she marvelled at the weird shapes of the modern buildings. It was like a completely new planet that they had travelled to - and only a train trip away from Sydney!

"Let's go find a place to stay," said Nathan. "Then we can take Alma out to her welcoming-home surprise."

After settling in and refreshing themselves, they left the city hotel and boarded a train once again. It was filled with young people squashed in so tight that Alma had trouble breathing.

Then to her surprise the train stopped out in the middle of nowhere at a little shed on the side of the rail-tracks.

Looking out across the open treeless plain, hundreds or maybe even thousands of people of all ages gathered in front of a huge stage.

As they joined the crowds and worked their way closer to the stage, Alma could see musicians setting up big black boxes, and testing instruments. Lights flashed and blinked, sending multitudes of rich bright colours out into the crowds. The sun disappeared over the distance horizon.

The sky changed gradually from light blue to purple and then on to a cloudless black. Millions of stars twinkled and the crystal clear moon shone down on the thousands below.

Everyone had thrown down blankets or rugs and lounged about without a care in the world. Strange music blasted out across the warm air.

Behind the main crowd, gas burners hissed, sausages sizzled and people danced in front of small tents. Large kegs pumped out frothing beer into plastic cups. Everyone sang and clapped and danced and laughed.

One band would play for half an hour before being replaced by another and then another. On and on it went, far into the night, and the early hours of the morning.

Suddenly the lights went out.

Everyone began to shout and heckle.

Small, hand-held flames and lights flickered over the whole area.

The morning sun hadn't yet shown itself over the horizon but it was beginning to glow faintly. While the dim pale glow could be seen far off in the distance, the overhead sky was still as black as ever.

"We want more... we want more...we want more," chanted the masses.

Then a small, silver star shot across the sky. It gradually grew in size as it darted towards Earth. When directly above the stage, it changed colour and hovered in the night sky. Now bright yellow and pulsating in and out, it again grew to the size of a white-hot miniature sun.

The whole crowd looked skyward.

Alma could sense the anxiety amongst the people, waiting and watching. What was it? She had never been to a open air concert. She didn't know what to expect.

The anxiety turned to suspense.

Alma, like many others, stood silently in anticipation.

Her heart fluttered at the silence - a complete contrast to the not-so-long-ago blasting music.

Bang!

Alma's body jerked in surprise.

The miniature sun exploded and shot out in every direction. Millions of sparkling lights flashed across the black sky.

Soon to follow were long fierce orange flames, fanning out from the white core as if a giant dragon breathed his angry fire into the atmosphere.

More explosions echoed around the concert area, drumming at the ground and shooting vibrations up through Alma's feet.

She stood frozen to the spot. She wanted to escape but her legs wouldn't move.

Long streams of light whizzed high up into the dark sky and then, after hanging in the night like little stars for a few seconds, whistled down towards the crowd in beautiful curves.

Slowly, the little white sun magically faded to a peaceful purple.

Gasps of delight could be heard throughout the masses as the purple expanded and engulfed the entire sky. It was as if someone up in the heavens had turned on a soft purple light.

As Alma looked at the sky she blinked in disbelief.

Then she peered at it with more effort, thinking she could see something, but not knowing exactly what it was.

A face!

She could now see the vague outline of a face that filled the whole of the sky.

The silver face appeared to be transparent and the long locks of blonde hair blended in to the purple background. Large wide eyes, filled with loving kindness, gazed down on the people. Her smile reached from one side of the horizon to the other.

Alma looked around at the other people near to her, just to make sure they were seeing the same as she was, and to make sure that she wasn't dreaming.

When she turned her eyes skyward again, the face instantly became recognisable.

"Debbie Clearwater!" she whispered. "It's Debbie!"

Admittedly, the face in the sky was so transparent, Alma felt that she was creating it, herself. It could be anyone's face. It was as if she had to use her will power to keep the face there in the sky. If her will power weakened, she subconsciously knew that the face would disappear.

But, from the look on other's faces, they could also see the image in the sky. So, how could it be? Were they seeing the same thing as herself?

An even stranger thing happened next.

A wave of love was thrown down from the sky.

It hit Alma, penetrating her whole body. Her inner self tingled as happiness spread throughout.

She danced inside herself.

While all this went on, Alma knew that she had to keep the image there in the sky. She doubled her concentration.

A soft melody caught her ears.

Then the most beautiful of voices began to sing. It could've been a love song but Alma wasn't sure. All that she knew was never before had she heard something so peaceful and tranquil.

Debbie didn't move her lips but the song seemed to come from her.

It must be by mind alone! No, it has to be telepathy, thought Alma. From the great mind in the sky, the silent voice reached down to each and every single mind in the crowd.

Alma felt so happy. Tears of joy filled her eyes and trickled down her cheeks.

The soft song stirred emotions throughout her body – beautiful emotions that she never thought possible.

It was as if Alma made up the words to the song and sang them to herself. But there was Debbie up in the sky! She could see her! It's not a dream, she told herself.

Alma didn't dare take her eyes from the shining silver face in the purple sky.

Suddenly the song died.

Then Debbie's lips moved, as she spoke for the first time.

"Goodnight," she whispered.

The face disappeared.

The purple faded into the morning glow of dawn.

The crowd of thousands stood gazing at the sky in silence.

Alma looked at the others standing next to her.

Everyone had wet eyes and smiling faces.

A man stood close by. He had a funny little black and white baseball cap on his head and wore thick glasses.

He turned to face Alma, as if sensing that someone was watching him. In slow motion, he took the glasses from his eyes.

Tears rolled down his face as he smiled at Alma.

PART THREE

CHAPTER FOUR

Nulla was crouching in the darkness, next to the massive sign at the entrance to the compound.

A truck engine could be heard far off down the road. The distant headlights stretched out along the highway and only just managed to throw a soft beam on the sign.

Nulla looked up and frowned as he read the dreaded words – 'Australwitz One'. Then he laughed at the smaller words underneath – 'Keep Out'.

Ronnie, Darcy and Freddie also crouched nearby, in the desert blackness. Their dark skinned bodies blended into the night.

They had been watching the compound for almost a week now. The stolen four-wheel drive was parked in a natural hollow in the desert sand, ready for a quick get-a-way. It remained hidden from the guards, yet was only a hundred or so yards from the entrance.

At last! The time had come to make a move. The guards had been doubled and security tightened since the last raid and escape. Only now, as Nulla had predicted, with limited government funds, the compound would have to resort back to their original guard numbers.

It had only been a matter of patience and now they could make their move.

One guard circled the front parking area, disappearing occasionally when he patrolled the residential houses off to the left.

Overhead lights lit up the white walls of the buildings.

The hospital, in the centre, stood higher than the prison to its left and the supply depot to the right.

Nulla could only just see the tourist shop as it hid in the shadows of a tree, on the other side of the supply depot.

Darcy tapped Nulla on the shoulder as the truck, quite a way off, could be heard switching down through the lower gears.

Nulla could read his mind and didn't bother to look back. They had waited for this moment and everyone felt the tension lift into excitement. He just kept his eyes on the compound and nodded his head slowly in agreement with Darcy.

Yes! It was time to go!

The four raiders, half-crouching, glided noiselessly across the highway, through the car-park and over to the far right corner of the tourism craft shop.

In the shadows of the night they watched the big white monster truck roar as it entered the car-park. With little difficulty, it swept in a wide circle and reversed in to a distance of no more than a few yards from the front of the supply depot.

Nulla gave the signal and they crept along the front of the tourism shop and hid in the entrance doorway. This is close enough, thought Nulla.

Within minutes the truck engine gave a final splutter. Apart from an occasional creak or groan from the long trailer, the compound car-park returned to its evil silence.

Then, as if appearing from the Dreamtime like a ghost, a dark figure walked up to the back of the truck. Keys jingled in the dark shadows. A heavy clang and a long metal screech followed.

Nulla could only just make out the security guard as he grunted and groaned, slowly pulling up the cellar doors.

"Gidday!" said the truck driver.

"Gidday yourself!" scowled the night guard.

Two men appeared from the far side of the truck and joined the guard.

"Leave you to it," continued the guard. "I'll be back in half an hour."

"Don't rush yourself, old-timer."

When the guard walked off, the two truckies lit up cigarettes and leaned against the back of the truck.

Nulla gave a hand signal to Darcy.

In seconds, a noise could be heard at the front of the truck.

"What was that?" said the driver, throwing his smoke to the ground.

"Yeah! I heard something too!" said his side-kick.

"Let's take a look. I never did like this place - what, with all the stories that get around."

"Yeah! It gives me the creeps too!"

"Ahhh!" yelled the first, as they headed off towards the front of the truck to investigate.

"Don't do that! I nearly had a heart attack then."

Both men could be heard laughing, pushing and shoving. Their voices faded as they walked off into the darkness.

Four shadows sprang forward, silently disappearing into the black pit of the cellar.

After half an hour of unloading, the truckies began cursing the night guard, as they waited for his signature on the documents.

"Go and get him!" said the driver, lighting another cigarette.

"I'm not going anywhere near that hell hole. I'll never be seen again!"

"I'm the driver. You're the lacky. It's your job to go get him."

"No way!"

The two men began wrestling and laughing again.

"What's going on?" yelled the guard, with keys jingling.

"Where the hell have you been? We finished unloading about ten minutes ago!"

"I got more important things to do than hang around here holding your hands," the guard grumbled.

Within minutes the steel trap-doors banged shut, keys jingled in the lock, and the truck roared as it headed out onto the highway.

Nulla stood dead still in the pitch-black cellar. When the truck's noise faded off into the distance, he raised his hands and reached out for the shelf.

Slowly he felt his way along the shelves, around the corner and up the stairs. With a little push the inside cellar trap-door lifted easily, to show the supply depot office on the ground-floor. He squinted as the light shot down into the cellar.

The others followed him up onto the shop floor of the supply depot, out through the rear double-doors, and into the maze of tin shacks.

Most of the inhabitants were asleep, but as the raiders light-footed their way along the dirt roads and through the back yards, scattered noises revealed that there were a few who were still awake - even at this late hour.

Nulla searched the dark sky above the roof tops as they kept to the shadows. It should be close now, he thought.

Then, all of a sudden, the great white branches of the tall eucalyptus tree loomed over a tin shack. Like a sacred landmark, the ghostly white tree trunk led the raiders to the famous little shack that belonged to Old Lloyd.

Nulla gave the smooth white bark a pat with his hand, thanking the magnificent tree for showing the way on this moonless night. Once again, after many years, he marvelled at the soft skin-like texture of the bark.

The four men could barely fit inside the small hut. Nulla lit the candle and shook Old Lloyd from a deep sleep.

"Where are they, old fella?" whispered Nulla.

"Out the back under the veranda," said Old Lloyd. He sat up on the edge of the bed and rubbed the sleep from his eyes. "There will be more in about a month."

"No worries," smiled Nulla. "See you then."

The men left Old Lloyd in the shack and went out back to collect the children – two boys and a girl of about seven to ten years of age.

Nulla knew that they would have been trained well and also knew that they understood what was expected of them.

Within minutes the group were silently jogging back towards the main complex.

Nulla surveyed the length of the complex. Although it was poorly lit, things seemed in order. He dashed forward and carefully opened the double-doors that led in the back way to the supply depot. When everyone was through the doors, he pulled them shut and turned the key. Instead of following the rest down into the cellar, he raced over to the office and switched off the circuit alarm.

Nulla then held the trap-door open and a beam of light shot down into the inky black hole. Darcy led the group over to the far corner where there was a small window at ground level.

He swung the window towards the inside and pulled at one of the steel bars that blocked the way out. They had had plenty of spare time to loosen it before tonight's raid. When it came loose he sent the children out first. Darcy and the other two followed. Then he reached in and pulled the window shut, replaced the steel bar and fled with the main group over towards the hidden four-wheel drive.

By this time Nulla had switched the alarm back on and climbed the stairs to the top third floor.

He was just in time to catch a glimpse of the shadows darting out through the car-park and over the highway to disappear into the desert.

The next move would be a little tricky. The timing had to be spot on. They would be able to use the same method again and again, if this mission went undetected.

He went to the far window, opened it and climbed out onto the narrow ledge.

Slowly he raised his body into a standing position while holding on to the outside of the window. Then he braced his hands hard against the sides of the brickwork as he carefully brought the window down using the toes of one of his bare feet.

Nulla's heart jumped into his mouth when he heard the whimpering down below. He glanced under his arm to see a dog wagging its tail and staring up at him.

It was one of the dogs from the residential houses of the permanent staff. The raiders had been regularly feeding the dogs at night and playing with them to gain friendship.

Nulla wasn't too keen on having a friend at the moment.

"Go away!" He whispered. "Go on!"

The dog moaned and cocked his head to the side, still wagging his tail.

He must've slipped his collar and decided to have a sniff around the car-park. Please go away, thought Nulla.

No such luck! The dog looked left, and then right, before sitting down. He was waiting for his friend to come down from the window.

This wasn't the time to stand around on a window ledge. He blindly reached out across the left-side wall and stretched his fingers until he found the drainpipe.

With a deep breath he let go and jumped sideways, towards the drainpipe. He managed to get both feet to find the steel pipe, but his right hand slipped as it reached for a grip.

His heart jumped into his mouth as he desperately held on with one hand while his body swayed back and forth. Nulla felt as if his fingers would soon be ripped from his hand.

Just as he swung his right arm up and secured a good hold, a voice could be heard from far over to the left.

"Hey! What are you doing over there?"

A faint beam from the guard's torch flittered about the ground searching the area around the dog.

The dog stood up, looked at the guard and wagged his tail furiously. Then he rolled over onto his back. With paws in the air, he waited for the guard to give him a pat.

"You naughty little fellow. Ah! I see. You slipped your collar. Come on. Let's get you back to your kennel before you get into trouble."

The guard walked off to the left and whistled behind for the dog to follow.

Nulla breathed a sigh of relief when the dog sprang to his feet and bounded off after the guard.

He started down the drainpipe.

Ten or so feet from the ground he was just about to jump and make a run for the four-wheel drive when the familiar whimpering returned. It startled Nulla so much that he felt as if he had shot up, out of his skin, into the air twenty feet.

Oh no!

He jumped and made a dash for the desert.

Within seconds, just as he felt freedom was in his grasp , a gunshot exploded from behind.

*

A woman in a white coat stood over him as he opened his eyes.

She shone a small light into the left eye. He tried to work out what was happening.

He felt the rush surging up from his stomach. Nulla jerked to a sitting up position. Vomit spewed from his mouth like a fountain, spraying the white hospital gown he was dressed in.

Then, the pure agony hit him. Exploding lights dazzled his eyes as the excruciating pain tore through his head.

Putting a hand to the back of his head, he touched a thick wad of cotton wool. The severe pain sent him spinning into unconsciousness.

The next time he opened his eyes, he saw the familiar prison cell bars.

A small man in a white coat walked into the cell and peered down at him.

Nulla tried to lift his head. A hammer blow of pain sent him into unconsciousness again.

A voice mumbled something from a distance.

Was someone trying to speak to him? Who is it? He couldn't see anything.

Nulla opened his eyes and discovered that the words were coming out of his own mouth. He had been mumbling in his sleep.

The cell bars were still there.

"Well, well, well. Look what the cat dragged in. It's about time, black boy. That was one hell of a good shot, hey? You must be blessed, to still be alive, after a shot like that," said Tom Martin, the prison manager. "We got a little surprise party waiting for you. You remember that little strange doctor in the white coat? Well, he is just itching for you to get better, real soon. You know why? Because he's gonna fry your brains out as soon as you're fit enough. And guess what? He promised me that I could come and watch! But, I'll tell you what I'll do as a favour just for you, black boy. You tell me where the secret hideout is, and I'll convince the good little doctor to take it easy on you. What do you say, black boy?"

Tom Martin leaned forward over Nulla, hoping to hear a whisper or something.

Nulla, despite the terrible pains in his head, lifted his head towards the prison manager.

Working up some moisture in his mouth, he spat with all the hatred of a hunted snake.

The last thing he saw was a big fist crash down upon his head.

PART THREE

CHAPTER FIVE

Alma looked out the window as the train headed north-west towards Broken Hill. The trees along the side of the track raced by in a blur, while the distant desert appeared to move in slow motion.

The feeling of homesickness started to lift, and the terrible churning in her stomach began to change to excitement.

Pictures of her father and mother, Nulla and Liddy, and many others took turns flashing through her mind.

The recent mental image picture of Lemmy's face returned again and again. A feeling of loss came over her and she swallowed hard.

She looked at the new watch on her wrist - a present from Lemmy when they said their goodbyes. She wondered if she would ever see Atty and Lemmy again.

This is the right thing to do, she told herself. It is time to go back to the caves. She laughed. There was no point in thinking about returning to 'Australwitz One'. There's no telling what would happen if she was discovered by those black traitors - Loo and Fish. They would surely hand her over to the doctor for punishment.

Maybe it would be better to go back to the caves, stay there for awhile, and then sneak in to see her family later. She thought about her mother and longed to see her warm friendly face.

The train pulled into Broken Hill.

Not far to go now, she thought. Soon she would see Nulla's smiling face. The mental pictures of the caves and the secret paradise brought a broad smile to her face.

As Alma walked from the train station she wriggled uncomfortably in Lemmy's tight clothes. She was still too close to The Law to change back into her own gear.

Walking down the main street of Broken Hill, Alma tried to make a decision about her next move. To go straight to the caves or to spend one more night in a soft bed - what would it be?

She glanced at a pretty dress in a shop window. An old woman walked past and stared at her. Alma could've have sworn that the old woman turned her nose up at her, as she passed.

That's it! Alma couldn't help but react to the snub.

She defiantly stepped up onto the veranda of the first hotel. Within five minutes she was looking out a first floor bedroom window down at the main street.

The town's main street was busy - cars zooming by, dogs and children running along the footpath, people shopping. She pulled a chair to the window and watched the white man's civilisation until the sun went down.

Alma had decided to have an early night and head out into the desert at first light. But after a quick bite of fruit and biscuits, she lay awake thinking about the town's noises drifting up from down below.

It was the last time she would be near a town, she thought. What the heck! Alma threw Lemmy's tight clothes on again and headed for the door.

On the way, along the hallway of the first floor, she passed an open doorway. The room was full of people! There must've been at least ten people in there!

A sign above the door showed her it was the guest's lounge room. She stopped and decided to linger, to find out what the attraction could be.

She stepped inside the room and leaned against the wall next to the door.

The guests were seated and facing a television screen, but didn't appear to be interested in what was on the screen. They sipped at drinks and chatted away to each other.

One or two of the guests looked her up and down but seemed to be more interested in the time on their watches.

It was then that Alma caught the sight of a man blocking the doorway. He must've followed her in. She could instantly feel the nervous energy course through her body from head to toes. Sweat appeared on her face.

She glanced at the man. He was staring straight at her.

"Excuse me, miss," said the uniformed policeman, "could you step out into the hall for a minute?"

Alma gave him a confused expression.

"I just want to ask you a few questions. Nothing to worry about, I assure you," continued the officer.

Alma found it difficult to support her shaking legs as she followed him out into the hall.

Not now! Not after all the travelling! Surely luck wouldn't run out this close to freedom!

"Could I ask what your name is, miss?"

"Lemuria," said Alma in her best American accent.

"And your last name and address?" continued the policeman.

Alma took a deep breath and tried to gather all her courage. She pulled out Lemmy's ID card and held it up in front of his face.

The policeman peered at the blurred photo on the ID and then glanced at Alma.

"Sorry, Lemuria. But I have a job to do. Thank you for your time. I hope you enjoy your stay in our country. Anything I can do..." The policeman stopped mid sentence and poked his head back around through the door at the hushing and shooing going on in the television room.

"It's time for the special news bulletin. You better go and get a seat," said the policeman, pointing into the room. "After you."

"Shoosh!" said an old woman seated at the front.

"Be quiet!" said another in the middle row.

Alma's knees wouldn't stop shaking as she walked stiffly to the back of the room and leant against the wall.

All eyes looked towards the television.

"Good evening," said the news reader on the television. " Earlier today we had an update on the current scene in the USSF of America regarding the imprisonment of psychiatrists.

"As you are aware, the debate on whether Australia should follow America's example had come to a standstill.

"That is, until now. Here is an urgent speech from Mister Geoff Whitman, leader of the Ned Kelly Party."

A middle-aged man with white hair and big black bushy eyebrows flashed onto the screen.

"Good evening. The Coalition Government headed by the Australian President, Mister Malcolm Don, has been dissolved due to a vote of no confidence. According to our constitution, a suitable deputy takes control as a caretaker until a general election can be held within the following six months.

"The reasons for the vote of no confidence and dismissal will now be given.

"If a government can be proven, beyond a doubt, to be incompetent and a danger to the welfare of the Australian public, then that government should be dismissed.

"Without public consent, the coalition government had just last night secretly passed a new law. This law would have allowed psychiatrists to go ahead with plans to surgically implant ID micro-chips into the skull of every new born baby, to have the power for compulsory drugging of school children, and to use electric shock therapy on any individual without that individual's agreement.

"All this would have gone through without public awareness. That is, until today's exposure of a recent crime committed by the psychiatric association.

"Today a video tape was sent to the media by an anonymous person. The video shows an attempted cover-up of the murder of a fourteen-year-old girl. She had been under the care of psychiatric doctors.

"This crime was a cold-blooded, cruel murder.

"The worst thing about this is that the government tried to use psychiatry as a control mechanism, to control the masses.

"The President of the USSF of America is currently reviewing the 'Brain Theory' of Psychiatry. We will be watching their progress and carrying out our own investigations.

"There will be more data given to you as this unfolds. The recent behaviour by the coalition government and psychiatrists shows treachery of the worst kind. This 'Brain Theory', including associated mental therapy, was an attempt to satisfy a greed for power and money.

"We have data coming in from American research. This research has been underway for some time.

"Tonight, as I speak, all psychiatrists will be sent to remand prison to await trial. For those few who will undoubtedly refuse to believe this, I will leave you with a replay of the video handed in today.

"Judge for yourselves!"

Alma watched the video of the young girl lying on the hospital table. The film showed the girl alive, before the ECT treatment, and dead after it. A small psychiatrist, in a white coat and spectacles, stood over the young girl.

Then the fake video was shown.

That's the doctor from the compound! It's him! Alma's attention went out across the desert to her family.

It was true! Liddy, at the caves, was right in what she had said. It was true what they have been doing to her people.

If the psychiatrists are in prison, the compound should be safe to visit.

Alma felt an urgent need to go home. She wished to see her parents, and now it appeared that she would be able to.

Sleep was impossible. Just before dawn she headed out along the highway in her own clothes - boots, short pants and t-shirt. It was good to get out of Lemmy's clothes.

Another family of tourists picked her up on the outskirts of Broken Hill.

The sun rose over the horizon as they headed for the compound.

Before long she was waving goodbye as they continued on down the highway after dropping her at the front gate of the compound.

It felt strange to look at the compound from outside.

An army truck stood in front of the hospital. Two soldiers leant against the front mudguards.

A crowd of Whites and Blacks gathered out the front of the tourism shop.

As Alma approached, she glanced in the back of the army truck. Two men and two women, in white coats, sat on the floor. Their hands were behind their backs, handcuffed.

Two soldiers brought a stack of small boxes and papers from the hospital and threw it all into the back of the truck.

The big ugly green truck jerked forward when the engine started up. Alma squinted through a low-lying cloud of dust as it roared off out onto the highway.

The Aboriginal Council members loaded up their four-wheel drives with whatever they could get their hands on. Loaded to the maximum with children and dogs, cupboards and suitcases, the vehicles moved off down the highway.

Council members glanced at the milling crowd as they passed by.

"Scum!" shouted someone amongst a group of blacks, and two others shook their fists at the cars and caravans as they filed out onto the highway.

Some-one picked up a rock and threw it after them.

Alma joined the crowd in front of the shop.

"Alma!" shouted a girl.

"Mary!"

They hugged and smiled.

"We thought something terrible had happened to you. Where have you been?" said Mary, a thin girl about the same age as Alma.

"Went walkabout," giggled Alma.

"Walkabout?" laughed Mary. "Your mum is in a terrible state with worry. She thought you must've ended up in the hospital and then disappeared like the others."

"It was something I had to do. I'll go see her in a while. She'll be alright."

"What about all this, hey?" Mary covered her eyes from the overhead sun and pointed at the departing vehicles. "Some say that the Council members were pocketing huge profits from the shop and the government handouts, while we scrounged and lived in tin shacks inside.

"They are running scared."

Mary then pointed back behind her to the tourism craft shop.

"The manager did a runner half way through the night. The soldiers told us that the shop is ours, to do whatever we please. They also said that there will be bulldozers coming out in the next few days. They're going to rip down the electric fences!"

Another girl, standing close by, joined them.

"Hi, Alma!" she said.

"Hi, Dot!" Alma replied.

"Where've you been?"

"Visited the city," said Alma. "What's going to happen here?"

"The soldiers turned the electricity off this morning," said Mary. "And they let everyone out of the prison and closed it down. They just took the psychiatric staff away in their truck. Locking them up! Fancy that! The soldier said that the medical doctor is in charge of the hospital until our people sort out what we want to do. It's all happening so fast! Isn't it exciting?"

"Yeah!" added Dot. "He said we can go anywhere we like. The restrictions have ended. We can go to the city! The coast! The west! Anywhere! And Whites can come here if they want."

Alma told the girls about the television speech last night in Broken Hill. A group of blacks had gathered to listen and were soon running off to spread the word.

Alma and Mary walked into the tourism shop. Weird! Look at this place. Alma smiled at Mary. She could tell that Mary had the same thoughts by the look on her face.

Neither of them had ever been in the sales side of the shop. White tourists walked around studying all the craft work as if nothing had changed.

Black folk were behind the counter taking money and chatting away to the customers.

Alma spotted a couple of emu eggs sitting on a shelf. She recognised her carving on one of the black eggs. Since her walk through the desert with Nulla and being with the people from the caves, a strong bond had developed with the animals of the land.

Now she wished for these animals to be left alone and their eggs to be left alone and for them to flourish like in the old times.

Suddenly Alma could feel someone staring at her from behind. When she swung around, her mouth widened in a big smile.

"Liddy!"

"Alma! I thought it was you. I just happened to look out the window and thought I was imagining it when I saw you standing there in the car-park."

Liddy wasn't smiling. She went on:

"Something horrible has happened. It's Nulla. He's in hospital next door. We were keeping a watch on this place ever since he was caught on a raid.

"When the soldiers turned up and took those doctors away, we came over and found him in a hospital bed. You better come quick. It's not looking very good."

As Alma and Liddy walked down the hospital corridor, two dark men and a nurse came out of a room.

Darcy and Freddie, naked except for string belts around their waists, hung their heads when they saw Alma.

Darcy then glanced at Alma and said:

"It's too late. He is no longer with us. He has gone elsewhere."

He didn't stop. Freddie never bothered to look up, but followed Darcy outside.

"I'm sorry. We did everything we could to try to save him. He died peacefully," whispered the nurse.

It was as if all the heat in her body had been instantly sucked out. Alma shivered uncontrollably as icy hands touched her insides. A heavy emotion hung in her throat like ice.

Her eyes welled up with water and her nose began to drip. Her arms and legs were lifeless - dead.

Liddy was saying something to her but Alma couldn't hear. Then Liddy grabbed her arm and led her into the hospital room.

It's not true. It's not true. This is a terrible dream. It's not true. I don't believe it.

No matter how many times Alma wished it not to be true, there in front of her lay Nulla's body.

His eyes were closed and he looked like he was asleep.

A white bed sheet stretched over his body up to his neck. His head rested to the side and his long black hair covered part of his face.

Liddy walked closer, bent over and kissed him on the forehead. Tears were in her eyes as she grabbed Alma's hand before leaving the room.

"I'll give you a minute by yourself before I'll have to ask you to leave," whispered the nurse.

She pulled the curtain closed and left Alma standing beside the bed.

Slowly she sat down on the edge of the bed. She picked up his hand and shook her head.

No. It's not true. Let me wake up. This is a terrible trick to play on me. It's not true. It's just a dream.

His hand was already cold.

"Nulla. It's my fault," whispered Alma. "You wouldn't be here if I had stayed. I was a selfish, stupid little girl. Please forgive me. I'm sorry."

Alma leaned down and put her cheek to his.

A flash of anger surged up inside her.

"You are not going to leave me," said Alma, lifting her head and looking up at the ceiling.

For some reason she glared up at the ceiling. Without being fully aware of what she was doing, she searched the ceiling for something. Something invisible could be felt. What was it?

"Nulla! Come back here! Come back to this body! Now!" yelled Alma at the top of her voice.

"Nulla! Come back here and take control of this body! Right now!" she yelled even louder.

For an instant she thought she felt something approach the body. She couldn't describe what it was, but could only feel it. She knew that something definitely had happened, but the body lay there, still, motionless.

"Stop being so stupid," Alma scolded herself. "He's dead! Stop imagining things. Let him go."

She cried into Nulla's cold face.

"I'm sorry, but you'll have to go now," whispered a nurse from the opened curtain.

Alma turned and stood up. She couldn't look at the nurse. Lost in a deep despair, her legs carried her numb body down the corridor.

What would she do now?

Alma wanted to find the nearest gun or knife or whatever, and end her life so that she could join Nulla - wherever he was.

It was her fault. And she would have to live with that for the rest of her life. If only she had stayed at the caves, he would be alright. He wouldn't be lying back there, dead.

A voice from behind echoed down the corridor.

Deep within her own little world, Alma didn't take any notice at first. But then the voice grew louder and nearer.

"Excuse me. Excuse me. Something has happened! He's alive! He's breathing and he has a pulse! It's a miracle!"

It was the nurse!

She had a strange look on her face which gradually changed into a big beaming smile.

Alma snapped out of her torture and raced back into the room.

Nulla fluttered an eyelid.

Alma put her ear next to his mouth and watched his chest for signs of movement.

"He's breathing! What happened?"

She looked behind to find the nurse smiling.

An overwhelming joy spread throughout Alma's body and she broke into an ear-wide smile.

Alma kissed Nulla on the cheek.

All she could whisper was:

"You came back. You came back."

PART THREE

CHAPTER SIX

Old Lloyd sat beside his campfire. Stars filled the dark sky and the moon spread silver light over the compound.

Smoke drifted up into his eyes but that didn't worry him. He continued to stare at the battered old photograph in his hand.

It was a picture of his wife.

No matter how many times he brought out that old photo, a beautiful feeling overcame him. He shook his head slowly.

She had made many sacrifices in the past mainly because he had asked her to make them. That final sacrifice had parted them forever, or what seemed like forever.

He threw the picture into the fire and watched the pretty smiling face disappear. From beauty, to black, to red, to white, and then to grey as the fire destroyed the last memory of her.

There! It has been done.

All connections to this world have been cut.

Old Lloyd picked up the spear that lay beside the campfire. He stood up and brushed his naked body down - cleaning off leaves and dirt that had stuck to him.

As he looked up at the multitude of stars in the sky, a smile stretched across his face.

"My final duty calls," he said to the universe above him.

Some people might consider this last duty to be the ultimate sacrifice. But it's no big deal to me, thought Old Lloyd.

Walking down the silvery road, he scanned through his past. There were good times and bad. The last lot of children he had trained, yes - a good bunch. They wouldn't need to stay at the caves. They could come back to live with their families. Now that the electric fences were down and the crazy doctors gone, things would be different.

He glanced here and there at the night shadows as the dirt track ahead of him shone in the light of the moon.

After some time he stopped and took a deep breath. He turned to his right and looked at an old shack, not much different to his own. Squaring his old shoulders, he gripped his spear and walked around the side of the shack to the backyard.

Old Egbert, the black sorcerer, sat next to his campfire. Smoke covered his face but Old Lloyd knew him, even at that distance.

The old black magician slowly opened his eyes, as if from a deep trance. Firelight flickered across the scarred withered body. White ash stripes covered his chest and face.

Old Lloyd tried to recall the last time he had met this old devil. It had been many years since they had last seen each other - and fought!

His minions were no-where to be seen. Probably out doing some dirty work for the evil old master.

The white sorcerer walked out into the middle of the yard and raised his spear to shoulder height. Naked and painted white with stripes of ash, he waited calmly.

Old Egbert slowly got to his feet. He was a carbon copy of the other – naked, covered in ash, and holding a spear.

As he approached, an evil presence could be felt but not seen. Thick, black energy filled the night atmosphere. Old Lloyd could sense the lost souls entrapped by this parasite. Ghouls and demons were here too - following the evil one wherever he went.

The two sorcerers stood a few yards apart.

Old Egbert lifted his spear to shoulder height as well.

They looked into each other's eyes, trying to find a weakness that could be used to advantage.

Old Lloyd gazed into the fierce snake eyes. He looked past them searching for the inner being.

He isn't even in his body, but somewhere close by, he thought. He expanded his attention to the surrounding area and picked up a presence, hovering about twenty feet directly above.

Without warning Old Lloyd thrust his spear into the groin of the sorcerer and ripped down through the genitals.

The challenger had the right to make the first move.

A groan! A gush of blood!

According to tradition, it was the other's turn now.

Old Egbert pulled back and let it go with full force.

Now there was blood streaming from Old Lloyd's groin, but no groans came.

Both men lifted theirs spears high into the air and shook them.

Then Old Lloyd stabbed at the other's upper leg.

Old Egbert retaliated with a similar stab.

The spears went high into the air again.

Taking turns, they worked on the legs. Then the stomach and chest were attacked.

Blood flowed but both men stood their ground.

It was Old Lloyd's turn and as he pulled back the bloodied spear ready for the strike, his enemy lunged forward. The tip of the spear slammed into Old Lloyd's left eye. With a flick, the eyeball popped out and hung from the socket.

Old Egbert quickly jabbed for the other eye before his enemy could recover from the first stab.

According to tradition this was the sign of a coward and therefore gave Old Lloyd the right to deliver the final blow before the fight was due to finish. But! He had to be quicker than his opponent.

Old Egbert's spear was already on its way.

As his spear penetrated the right eye, sending red hot pain into the centre of his head, Old Lloyd thrust with all the might he could muster.

It had been a split second to judge direction. His body was already weak from the many wounds and continual flow of blood.

He heard the thud but couldn't see because the enemy's spear had struck home, leaving him sightless. Twisting and pushing harder into the flesh of his opponent, Old Lloyd fell forward. His legs were so weak they were unable to support his body.

In what felt like slow motion, his knees hit the dirt. The spear was still jammed in his eye socket.

Why hadn't Old Egbert pulled it back for the final blow?

Old Lloyd yanked the spear from his eye and threw it to the ground. Then he crawled forward to search for the enemy.

Where was he?

The area in front gave no clues. Had he disappeared?

Old Lloyd couldn't see. Both eyes were out.

A thud!

Old Lloyd gasped as a terrible pain pierced his heart. He grabbed at the spear but couldn't pull it from his chest.

Slowly he ran his hand along the slippery shaft of the spear and stopped when he felt the enemy's hand.

A body fell forward, gasping for air.

Old Lloyd ran his hands over the chest of the enemy and found that his own spear had struck the intended target.

He then fell forward, completely exhausted and drained of life.

Both men, kneeling in the sand and leaning against each other, reached for a strangle hold around the neck.

As they fell to one side and crashed into the sand, the last drops of blood flowed from their hearts. Both men continued squeezing each other's throat.

The darkness of the night zoomed in toward the blood splattered bodies.

In an instant Old Lloyd floated out of his body to watch from above. He knew that Old Egbert had already disappeared into the void. He also knew that he would soon follow.

One last look at his withered old body. It had served him well, he thought.

A muscle twitched in one of the legs.

The camp fire crackled in a final burst of flame before smoke spiralled up into the air. Slowly the grey stream of smoke drifted off along the ground towards the back trees.

Old Lloyd glanced back at his body. One final look.

With his mind's eye, he penetrated the flesh and envisioned the white bones. Then he put his attention on the decayed spirits that slept there, hugging tight to the bones.

In sudden fright at being discovered, the little spirit-beings scattered into the dark night.

All that's left now, thought Old Lloyd, is the cellular spirit energy. This will soon gradually fade away and be absorbed elsewhere.

Time to leave this planet, he smiled.

What a good feeling! To be free! And start a new adventure!

PART THREE

CHAPTER SEVEN

Doctor Curr sweated in the back seat of the four wheel drive jeep.

He glanced over his shoulder to look back along the road. Good! No one following us, he thought.

When he looked to the front once more, Loo was staring at him through the rear vision mirror. Loo smiled as he sped along the road and Doctor Curr shifted uneasily in the rear seat.

There were no signs of police or army vehicles on the road. Doctor Curr felt confident, and even though he had taken his daily injection that morning, he threw a handful of tablets down his throat just to help things along.

They had been driving for hours now. The air conditioned luxury jeep kept the summer heat out but the burning sun still manager to penetrate the tinted windows. Doctor Curr adjusted his suit coat, that hung from the hook above the side window, to keep himself in shade.

Fish sat in the front passenger seat - his head bobbing and lolling about as the jeep bounced along the back roads.

Doctor Curr wished he could doze for awhile but knew it would be impossible to get any sleep under this threat of capture - not unless he took some really strong tranquillisers.

His line of thought wandered to Doctor Hapsburg, the Australian President of Psychiatry. Surely they caught him. He must be in prison. The army would have made him the first priority.

Doctor Hanover, the International Psychiatric President, would be safe and on his way back to Germany, the Fatherland.

Doctor Curr smiled. Just the thought of the Fatherland gave him a very reassuring secure feeling. He imagined what it shall be like when he returns soon - the picturesque hills and valleys, the glorious cities and the modern state-of-the-art psychiatric hospitals.

Yes! He could finish the last couple of years in the Fatherland before retiring. Australia can go to hell!

Loo had taken the south roads until they reached the Murray River, crossed the border into Victoria, and followed the back roads that meandered along with the river.

Then they crossed the border, back into New South Wales, and headed up into the Blue Mountains - in the south-east corner of Australia, slightly below Sydney.

Not long now, smiled Doctor Curr.

The pills were beginning to work. His mouth lost all sensation and dried up. A feeling of ecstasy swept through his body. He wanted to lie down on the seat and let the wonderful experience overwhelm him completely but knew he couldn't. To let these two black fools control his destiny would be utter madness.

All of a sudden the jeep screeched to a halt.

"What's going on?" Doctor Curr panicked, expecting police sirens and army helicopters.

"Idiot!" Loo shouted. He pulled his oily leather hat from his head and smashed it into his partner's face.

"What did you do that for?" Fish yelped.

"Give me the map." Loo ripped the paper out of Fish's hands. "Got to do everything myself, haven't I?"

"It's not my fault. I don't know this neck of the woods. Too many turns and side roads. Too many trees and not enough signs." Fish shielded his face from an expected back-hand but it didn't come.

Loo traced a finger over the map, then threw the crumpled up remains at Fish. He slammed the gear stick into first, shook his head in disgust and sped off up the winding mountain back-road.

Doctor Curr fell back into the seat and relaxed.

It will all be over soon, he told himself. Just hang on a few more hours - just a few more.

He recalled the strange phone call in the middle of last night. And the deal he had made with the ex-politician. One hundred thousand dollars for a false passport and airline ticket. Twenty thousand dollars, to pay Loo and Fish for the getaway.

Either that or twenty years in an Australian prison! Not on your life!

Damn these human rights fools! We were so close to completing the Australwitz Programme and so close to finalising the political infiltration programme. Our men were already in the top political positions. Just a few more weeks and everything would have been ready for the take-over.

The whole population would've been implanted with the micro-chip within a number of years. My work would've been finished. Extra bonus! Retirement around the corner!

Now what?

Damn those human rights activists.

The jeep stopped suddenly and Loo stepped out.

"Is this it?" Doctor Curr called after him.

"Need fuel." Loo stuck his head in past the top of the seat and whispered, " It's up the road a few miles. Twenty thousand - ten thousand a piece. Right?"

"Yes! It's all been arranged." Doctor Curr sighed in irritation.

"Cash! No cheques."

"Yes! Of course!"

Loo smiled at Fish and went to fuel up.

A few miles up the road, hidden amongst dense forest, they came to a magnificent holiday house. The door was unlocked and no people were inside.

After resting for an hour or so, a great big black car rumbled into the driveway. It pulled up at the front of the house, motor still running, and waited.

Loo and Fish, rifles in hand, walked out and stood on the porch.

Doctor Curr hurried down to the car and was handed an envelope through the window.

With relief, Doctor Curr stared at the contents - a passport and an airline ticket.

The relief quickly turned to panic and confusion.

"The money? Where's the thirty thousand in small bills?" he said to the driver.

Wrap-around dark sun glasses hid the driver's eyes. Doctor Curr instantly took a dislike to the man - greasy black hair combed straight back, big bent nose, thin moustache and cigarette hanging out of the mouth.

The driver didn't look at him, or reply.

"The money?" Doctor Curr looked at the driver and then opened the envelope and searched again. "It's not here!"

Boots crunching along the gravel driveway made Doctor Curr's heart flutter. When he turned, Loo was casually walking towards the car. The sun cast a shadow over his dark face, half hidden under the rough leather hat.

Loo smiled as he pulled the rifle down from his shoulder and pointed it towards the car.

"I can get the money sent to you, Loo." Doctor Curr shoved the envelope into the pocket of his white coat. "There's been some mistake."

Loo chuckled and shook his head slowly from side to side.

"He must've stolen it!" Doctor Curr stepped away from the car and pointed at the driver. "The money is supposed to be in the envelope! Look! It wasn't sealed when he gave it to me. He must've taken it!" Doctor Curr pulled the envelope out again and held it up to Loo.

Loo didn't look at it but stared at the driver.

The driver, still looking forward said:

"Look mate - I'm going to count to ten and then I'm going to drive off. If you get in I'll take you to the airport as planned. That's what I'm being paid for. I didn't take your money. One, two, three, four…"

Loo flicked the safety off and pointed the rifled at the driver.

"Get out, whitey."

The car tyres screeched and instantly surged forward.

Loo casually took aim and fired two shots before the car had reached the front gate. The back end of the car dropped in the dust and the wheels dug into the soft dirt.

A black figure darted from the car and ran along the road a short distance before taking a dive in amongst the trees.

Loo jerked a thumb at Fish and then glanced at Doctor Curr. Fish stepped down from the porch and pointed his rifle at the little man in the white coat. Doctor Curr could feel his legs shaking.

Grief welled up inside his chest as he watched his foolproof plan slipping away.

Loo slung the rifle over his shoulder and strode off down the driveway.

Within minutes a noise came from the forest - a rapid fire that sounded like a machine gun.

Then a single shot echoed around the forest.

Loo appeared shortly after and walked back towards the car. He stopped and searched it but soon returned empty handed, except for the rifle.

Doctor Curr looked around but there was no-where to run. To try dashing for the jeep would be stupid. Loo would fire a shot before two steps were taken.

He was at a loss on what to do next.

He dropped to his knees in the dusty driveway.

"Please Loo, listen." He cried, "I can get the money. Just take me to the airport and when I get to Germany, I'll send a hundred thousand or whatever you want. Please believe me."

"Shut up, weasel." Loo laughed and pointed the end of the barrel at the head of the doctor. "I knew it. I just knew there would be a double-cross."

"I promise Loo. I didn't try to double-cross you. Take the jeep. It's worth ten thousand or more - it's yours!"

"You're damn right it's ours." Loo turned to Fish and they laughed and sneered at the disgusting spectacle in front of them. "I've seen little rabbits with more guts than you."

Doctor Curr held up his hands and began to cry as Loo put the barrel next to the side of his head.

Loo pulled the trigger and the rifle made a clicking sound as the firing pin hit an empty chamber.

Doctor Curr jumped in fright.

"Please, please Loo. Don't do this. I can sort out all this mess."

"I wouldn't even waste a bullet on this piece of dog meat," grumbled Loo.

The big black man turned as if he was going to walk away. Then with a jerk of his arm, he up-ended the rifle and rammed the butt into the side of the doctor's head.

Light vanished instantly.

Doctor Curr fell to the ground.

No pain! Just blackness!

He tried to open his eyes but couldn't.

Loo was saying something - what?

"I'll bet my half of the jeep it only takes one stomp."

"I bet it takes three."

A boot slammed down hard on the doctor's head. He could feel his skull caving in. In an instant, an almighty pressure from inside forced his eyes opened. A light flashed and then suddenly disappeared.

Pain ripped his head apart.

Silence.

Confusion followed. A floating sensation took over.

What's happening?

He could only experience blackness but at the same time it seemed as if he began to float or drift away from his body.

Was he dead? Unconscious? Or semi-unconscious?

Within seconds the floating sensation stopped.

Doctor Curr realised that he had travelled to somewhere out in space. No time involved! Not even a split second! He had been transhipped to some sort of space station deep in outer space in an instant!

Wait a minute! He recalled that this experience was familiar - as if he had been here before, many times.

A voice boomed.

"Number 413655850998."

An electronic blast hit him with an unbelievable force.

He still couldn't see anything!

A light flashed.

Blankness! It was as if his mind had been disintegrated by the continual spurts of powerful electronic energy thrown at him.

Pictures began to appear.

Unfamiliar scenes of roads, houses, trees and people flashed through his mind.

"Who was he? Where was he? What was happening to him?"

Strange pictures of people engaged in sexual activity whirled before his mind.

Pictures of people worshipping a statue appeared next.

Pictures of angels and dogs and cars flooded in.

Dizziness overwhelmed him.

He went to sleep but knew that it wasn't really proper sleep.

A woman screamed.

"Push! Push! Breathe deeply and slowly. One more push."

Another scream!

A magnetic force sucked him down.

A hospital! A woman giving birth to a baby!

Doctor Curr let out a scream as a gush of cold unfriendly air filled his lungs.

He shivered in the cold draft.

A nurse covered him with an uncomfortable white towel.

"There, there, little baby … everything's alright."

"It's a little girl!" said the nurse.

PART THREE

CHAPTER EIGHT

Alma and Nulla stood under the shade of the old eucalyptus tree, out in the front yard of her home. It was just after the middle of the day.

"Are you sure you're fit enough for the celebration dance tonight?" asked Alma.

Nearly two months had passed since Nulla lay half dead in hospital. His recovery had been remarkable.

A slight breeze ruffled her long silky black hair. She gazed into Nulla's strong dark eyes.

Many of the people from the caves had moved into the settlement and were now busy re-educating the compound dwellers in bush survival. They were allowed to go wherever their whim took them. Gone were the electric fences and psychiatric torture and prison.

The leaves up above rustled in the cool air and cast splotches of shadows over Nulla's near naked body.

"Yes, I should be alright now," smiled Nulla. "Thanks to your mother's efforts."

"Don't worry about her and dad's teasing. They don't really mean it."

Nulla laughed out loud.

"Yeah! Sure they don't want to see us married as soon as possible," he teased.

"I wouldn't marry you anyway," said Alma, playfully pushing him in the chest.

"We'll soon see about that," said Nulla. He grabbed Alma's arm.

"You're pretty sure about yourself, hey?" joked Alma.

Nulla continued to hold her tight and the look in his eyes became serious.

"Alma…," he began to say.

"Hey!" shouted her father, Frank Morgan. He walked along the sun beaten dirt track towards them. "What are you two up to?"

"What happened to your hands?" asked Alma, in shock.

Blood dripped from Frank's knuckles as he lifted his massive hands to see what all the fuss was about.

"Oh! That's nothing. Just a little exercise to keep an old bloke fit."

"Who was it? No-one from the caves, I hope?" asked Nulla.

"No. They're a good bunch. I ran into a couple of black bums in a fancy jeep. I've always had a bit of a feud with them as long as I can remember. They were drunk and tried to run me over, so I had to sort them out. And the best part is that they'll be there next week to have another go. It keeps me on my toes." Frank laughed and gave Alma a half wink.

She cringed but tried not to show it. Did her father find out about the desert ordeal with Loo and Fish? She had seen the two of them driving around the compound the past few weeks. Her father had never told her that they were old fighting rivals.

Frank was already on his way into the shack before Alma could look into his eyes to search for the truth.

"I better get cleaned up," said Frank as he disappeared through the door.

Later, as the sun faded and the night stars began to sparkle, people gathered around a huge fire.

Old George, the tribal elder from the caves, walked out into the centre and held up his hands.

The fierce light from the fire appeared to create an aura of flames that surrounded his body.

More than a thousand people sitting on the desert sand watched and waited. The night became silent except for the crackle of sparks in the massive fire.

Old George, satisfied he had every one's attention, began to speak:

"Here is a story passed down from a long time ago by the old people - our ancestors.

"This story says that once there were two Old People who are now a moon and a fish.

"Once, they were not a moon and a fish, but instead, they were men.

"When they were men, the fish was called 'Loolor'; and the moon was called 'Nullallandy'.

"Our ancestors said that this moon and fish were like men before, and that they could speak our language - just like you and me.

"Loolor, the fish, he had children and a wife; and Nullallandy, the moon, also had children and a wife.

"Loolor, the fish, he says: 'I'm going to die. I will die only once and not live forever.'

"And then he says: 'I'm going to leave my wife and children when I die. I'm going to be dead. I will die only once and not live forever.'

"Nullallandy, the moon, says: 'I'm not going to die forever. No, never. This is going to be a short death and then I will live again.'

"Loolor, the fish, then says: 'I'll never see my wife and children again. I will be dead forever.'

"Nullallandy, the moon, says: 'I'm going to die, and up there, I will turn into a moon. It will be a short death and then I will come down and live again', And then he says: 'You, Loolor, say that you are going to die and leave nothing behind but your bones. You say that you are going to die forever, so you die forever. Again and again, you will die, and again and again, you will say there is no more.'

"Loolor, the fish, then says: 'People will be like me - they will die once and be no more.'

"Nullallandy, the moon, says: 'No. People will be like me - they will have a short death, then live again.'

"Then the two men, Nullallandy and Loolor, turned into a moon and a fish, and the moon - as he said - he died a short death and lived again, and again. And Loolor, the fish, he died forever and nothing but his bones were left in the sand."

Old George looked over to Frank Morgan who at once started up the strange hollow sound of the didgeridoo.

The crowd joined in with rhythmic singing. Some swayed from side to side and chanted.

A group of clay-covered men sprang into the middle.

The fire blazed behind them as they danced and strutted about.

A ring of old women, at the front, chanted in time to the dance.

Alma sat close behind the old women. She thought she could recognise one or two of the dancers - maybe Darcy and Fred - but Nulla was not amongst them. Where was he?

Smoke filled the air. Dust rose up from the dry earth.

The clay-white skeletons stamped their bare feet harder and harder into the ground.

The singing and chanting gradually increased.

All of a sudden the dancers stopped.

The didgeridoo stopped.

The chanting stopped.

The men froze into statues.

Smoke from the fire covered their bodies.

More smoke drifted over the area.

An explosion threw sparks up into the night, and the smoke disappeared.

The dancers were no longer there!

The space was empty!

Silence.

People cautiously looked about to see what was going to happen next.

Alma nearly jumped out of her skin as a piercing scream broke the magic spell.

A figure leapt into the middle of the dance ground, in front of the fire.

White clay gave a hideous appearance to the figure - a mixture of a sorcerer and skeleton.

He stretched his arms wide and the didgeridoo started up with its primitive pulsating.

He swayed to the rhythm of the music.

The old women took up the mood with chanting and clapping.

Alma looked hard but couldn't decide if it was Nulla. It was difficult to tell with all those feathers, the frightening white skull and skeleton body.

The figure moved slowly around the fire at first, then circled wider - getting closer and closer to the crowd.

With arms still stretched wide and head almost motionless, his legs began to move faster. Then his knees would move in and touch before shooting out, then back in again.

The women clapped faster.

The knees moved in and out - faster and faster.

The figure dropped his head. A spirit bag appeared in his mouth and he bit hard into it when his head came up again.

A spear appeared in his hand and he let out a war cry.

The dancer had instantly been transformed in to a warrior in full rage.

Without warning he jumped into the crowd and roared like some sort of primeval animal.

The red evil eyes darted about, staring at the people.

Alma was terrified. She felt a strange sensation rip through her body. It was as if she had been asleep as a spirit inside her physical body and the warrior war cry had torn her out of an eternal trance. The terror slowly changed to peace, once the initial shock disappeared.

Then the figure leapt, as if flying, back to the space in front of the fire.

Arms stretched wide again, the figure restarted the dance. His knees vibrated in and out much more frantically now.

The women clapped faster to try to keep up with the dance but his legs were moving so fast now that they were almost a blur.

Alma couldn't believe what happened next. She strained to see better through the smoke.

The legs of the warrior had disappeared and the upper body seemed to slowly fade away to leave nothing but the flames behind it.

She blinked again and again but still couldn't see the figure.

It was as if the figure had melted into the fire!

The didgeridoo stopped.

The old women stopped chanting and clapping.

All noise stopped except for the crackle of the fire.

Its heat flowed out to mingle with the crowd.

And then the fire exploded!

A powerful heat blasted out in a circle.

Whoosh!

Alma could feel a strange energy building up inside her. She couldn't control it. Slowly it rose up inside towards her head and then she let go.

Like a volcano, she burst out through the top of her skull.

A burst of pure joy!

She looked down at her body still sitting amongst the crowd while she danced a dance of pure happiness.

Then another force seemed to join in with her dance high up in the dark night.

Hugging each other, they spirited through the sky like two comets in full flight.

It was Nulla!

But then someone called out to Alma.

She looked around but couldn't quite locate the voice.

Someone shook her shoulder.

"Alma! Wake up!" said the Aboriginal Tourist Shop Manager. "It's five o'clock. Go home."

Alma lifted her head.

Suddenly she became aware that she had fallen asleep at her workbench. She looked at the emu egg and then at the clock on the wall.

She realised she had been asleep for the last half hour.

"Go home Alma. And try to get some sleep tonight so you don't go to sleep tomorrow during work hours," said the manager. "I don't want to sack you but there are plenty of others prepared to work if you don't want to."

"Sorry," whispered Alma. She stood up and headed for the door.

As she walked down the dirt track of the compound she tried to remember her dream. Something about a dance and a fire and ... It was a blur and she couldn't quite put it all together.

That's strange! She was surprised because she had never gone to sleep at work before.

Alma walked down the dirt track, past her home and out over the main canal, to the lonely desert part of the compound.

She felt the urge to be alone.

Not walking in any particular direction, she soon found herself way up in the north section. She hadn't been in this section before.

The desert sand stretched for miles.

She kicked the warm sand from her sandals.

What's this?

A piece of plastic half buried in the sand!

Alma pulled at it.

It was a parcel.

She opened it up.

It was an old book!

THE   END

ISBN 155212767-2